D. Bowers

CW01425657

TERRORIST INVASION OF THE SOUTH OF ENGLAND

D. M. Bowers

Pen Press

First published in Great Britain by Pen Press

All paper used in the printing of this book has been made from wood grown in managed, sustainable forests.

ISBN: 978-1-78003-446-1

Printed and bound in the UK
Pen Press is an imprint of
Indepenpress Publishing Limited
25 Eastern Place
Brighton
BN2 1GJ

A catalogue record of this book is available from
the British Library

Cover design by Jacqueline Abromeit

To the Salisbury Family
and the friends I have made in the Meon Valley

Francis

I hope that you
enjoy my book

Dereen Bowers

Chapter One

It was beginning to rain as Annie Butler, better known to her friends as AB, arrived in the hospital car park. She parked the car and made her way to the main entrance of the hospital. The building looked sinister in the grey light of the winter gloom. Barbed wire covered its perimeter walls and the hospital gave the appearance of a prison. As she reached the main entrance gates that were guarded by a security guard he glanced briefly in her direction but he seemed only interested in the vehicles that were driving through the main gates.

Reading the direction boards she followed the route to the Admissions Department. Here the receptionist asked her to sit down and wait to be called. It wasn't long before she was summoned into a small room where her details were taken down and then she was given directions to Ward E6. The corridors echoed to the sound of her footsteps as she made her way to the lift. She felt that she had no control over her destiny. Ever since she first saw a consultant ten years ago she had wanted this operation but now it was imminent she was apprehensive. She had learned to live with the pain and, at the age of 72, wondered if she could afford the lengthy recovery period in her declining years. There was so much to do! Taking the lift to the third floor she realised that there was no turning back now!

The lift ground to a halt and she waited for the doors to open. Leaving the lift, AB followed the directions to the ward. All too soon she had arrived! It was a mixed ward. Men occupied one end and women the other and there was a nurses' station in the middle separating the two sexes. AB hesitated at the entrance, unsure whether to enter the ward. Nurses at the station glanced in her direction but made no move to come to her assistance and so, plucking up courage, she made her way down the ward to the nurses' station. AB had known that she would be going into a mixed ward and had politely said that she was unhappy with the situation but was assured that she would be in the female end of the ward and therefore there was no need to worry. Reaching the nurses' station she handed over the admittance letter. One of the nurses said she would take her to her bed to get her settled in. It was with some apprehension that she was led to the male section. At this point, AB was tempted to walk out and go home. She made her views known to the nurse who sympathised and said she would see what she could do. AB was near to tears but realised she could still go home. However, when the nurse returned she said that there would be a bed in the women's section later in the day but AB would have to stay in the waiting room until it was ready. Breathing a sigh of relief AB followed the nurse to the waiting room and, taking a seat, she tried to make the most of the situation. She took a book from her bag and began to read.

Unable to concentrate she glanced around her. The room was gloomy and the furniture was in need of updating. A television stood in one corner of the room but it did nothing to lift her depression. Glancing through the window AB could see a small green with several benches. The sky was overcast and the clouds were dark and foreboding. The day dragged on but, at last, a nurse came to take her to a bed. Once there, she had various tests in preparation for tomorrow's operation. Blood was taken, for use after the operation, because a large amount of blood would be lost and they would use AB's own blood to replace that lost. Once the tests were completed the curtains were pulled back und AB was able to get acquainted with the other patients and to take stock of her surroundings. It was rather gloomy as there were no windows on one side of the ward and where there were windows the wind rattled the panes of glass. AB noticed that many were sealed with black tape, presumably to stop the draughts. Some of the curtains had come adrift from their hooks and hung untidily from the rails. The ward was very hot and AB was glad that she had brought lightweight night attire. The other patients were a friendly bunch coming from various parts of the county. All were in hospital for orthopaedic operations. Some were recovering from surgery. Others, like AB, were awaiting operations. One elderly lady had been in hospital for a month while they built up her strength for a hip operation. During the evening the anaesthetist came to discuss with AB the various options for anaesthetics. He suggested an epidural as recovery would be quicker and AB agreed. By 8.00 pm everyone had settled down for the night. The night shift staff came on duty and the afternoon shift departed. Hot drinks were served to those patients who wanted them and then a male nurse wheeled in the drugs trolley. He proceeded to dispense drugs to those patients who required painkillers.

Soon the lights were dimmed and AB tried to shut out the noise of the machinery that was used to improve the blood circulation after operations. The ceaseless click-click made it almost impossible to relax. Also there seemed to be an endless stream of nursing staff walking up and down the ward and the banging of the fire door as nurses made their way to the staff room for coffee. Exhausted, AB eventually drifted into sleep but, all too soon, as the morning staff came on duty and the night staff departed, AB awoke. The drinks trolley was wheeled round but AB was not able to have food or drink and so she decided to go to the washroom. Taking her towel and toothbrush etc from the bedside cabinet she walked to the end of the ward and opened the door of the shower room. There was a shower in one corner and opposite the shower were two sinks. There were screens for those who wanted privacy. AB felt refreshed after her wash and returned to the ward to await her fate. The staff nurse came to tell her that she was number three on the ops list and it would probably be around 12.30 before she went down to the theatre. The ward became a hive of activity as more staff came on duty and the ward rounds began. The day staffs were a mixture of NHS, agency, army, navy and air force nurses. Two very young nurses came round with the drugs trolley – one army and one navy nurse. They handed out the drugs, took patients' temperatures and entered the data on the patients' charts that were kept in a pocket at the end of each bed. The physiotherapist came onto the ward and first called at the nurses' station to collect a list of patients that would be receiving his attention that day. The doctor did his rounds checking each patient's chart and taking note of the progress made.

AB tried to read but couldn't concentrate. She decided to write to her brother but only managed half a page because there was so much activity. Soon the lunch trolley arrived but for AB there was no meal. Ah well, only another hour, she thought, and the operation would commence. Strangely the time passed quite quickly. The nurse brought the white coat and stockings for AB to wear. She then checked the wristbands for allergies. This done, the nurse disappeared. Next the staff nurse arrived with the pre-med injection and AB drifted into inner calm. She was never aware of receiving the epidural injection. The last she remembered was being pushed along the ward on the bed and then entering the lift. AB vaguely remembered hearing a sawing noise that, no doubt, was bone being sawn away. It was like listening to a neighbour working on a DIY project. Eventually AB became aware that she was back in the ward. Not fully conscious she had a feeling of immense relief. The operation was over and she had survived. She had a drip supplying a pain-killing infusion and blood was being transfused into her veins. The slippers that helped the blood circulation were on AB's feet. The steady click-click of the machinery continued. At that moment all was well with the world and she drifted into sleep once more.

The voices of the night staff coming on duty drifted into her consciousness and the banging of the fire door brought AB to her senses. An Asian nurse wheeled the drugs trolley round and gave the patients their nightly fix. Hot drinks were offered as a nightcap and all the patients accepted the offer except for AB. Soon all the patients had drifted off into sleep. AB could now hear the conversation from the nurses' station even though she was some distance away. There were occasional bursts of laughter then the tone seemed to change. AB listened intently and managed to catch parts of the conversation. Words like 'finding the hot spot' and 'mighty explosion'. She didn't recognise the man's voice. Then she caught the sound of a nurse's voice that she did recognise.

'I couldn't do that to the old lady,' she said.

More laughter, then the man's voice again. AB strained to hear what was said but although she knew that something sinister was being planned she couldn't be sure what they had in mind. Sleep overcame her curiosity and she drifted off once again. She awoke some minutes later and found the male nurse by the side of her drip. He was shining a small torch on the tube containing the pain-killing drug. He moved the torch up and down. Suddenly AB realised that she was the old lady. The nurse was trying to ignite the contents of the tube. He was going to blow her up!

She pulled herself together and asked, 'What are you doing, you silly fool?'

'I not a silly fool,' he replied.

He left and returned to the nurses' station. More whispered conversation followed and then an angry voice shouted.

'Go home now, both of you, and don't come back.'

Running the length of the ward and laughing as they went the two nurses disappeared through the fire door with a crash. AB wondered if the danger was over. The whispered conversation gave her the impression that it wasn't. She seemed to be the only patient still awake. It dawned on her that there were terrorists in the ward. What was their aim, she wondered? There seemed little motive in destroying a hospital but perhaps that was not their intention. Were they suicide bombers?

The other patients slept on as fear began to take hold of AB. What should she do? She had to save everyone, but how? AB felt trapped by the apparatus that she was wired to and realised that she had to release herself to create a disturbance in order to attract the attention of nursing staff from the other wards. So with difficulty AB, recklessly, removed the clicking slippers from her feet and then disconnected the drips. As she did so blood spurted out and, although she was now free, she had to stem the flow of blood, as she couldn't afford to lose any more. She pulled the sheet from the bed and wrapped it round her leg.

In the bed opposite a patient stirred and AB realised that two other patients were now awake. It occurred to her that some of the patients might also be terrorists. Were those two involved or could they be trusted? She knew she must take a chance now, if she was to alert the genuine staff. So she called across to the patient in the opposite bed.

'Quick, fetch Staff Nurse. I'm losing a lot of blood.'

The patient climbed from her bed and hurried to the nurses' station. AB listened to angry voices as the terrorists realised their plan had been thwarted. A male nurse with an Irish accent arrived with a laundry trolley and quickly removed the soiled sheets. An Asian nurse replaced the slippers and reset the clicking machine. The blood was disposed of and the drip was not reconnected. Another nurse came to check the dressing on AB's knee and then, with a colleague, remade the bed with clean sheets.

Quiet descended once more and the sleeping patients slept on. AB was sure that she had stopped what may have been a disaster and felt quite smug. She forced herself to stay awake, not trusting the night staff and, finally, the day staff came on duty and began the daily routine. Everything seemed to be back to normal and AB relaxed.

A nurse arrived to change the dressing on AB's knee. She closed the curtains round the bed and began to prepare the equipment needed, carefully laying out each item.

Then, to AB's surprise she said, 'This will make you scream.'

AB was suddenly aware that the nurse was threatening her. Determined not to scream she took a deep breath and gritted her teeth. She felt a searing pain around the wound but managed not to utter a sound. The nurse gave a menacing grin and, as she redressed the wound she said mockingly, 'There you didn't scream, did you?'

AB said that she would expect two nurses next time as she didn't trust her to dress the wound alone. The nurse withdrew and the curtains were opened to the relief of AB. In the next bed the patient was still asleep after her operation. She was snoring loudly and AB realised that she was not going to get any peace for some time. The doctor had started his rounds and very soon came to see AB. He looked at the dressing and checked AB's chart then moved on to the next patient. A nurse came to give AB a wash and to assist her to get dressed and soon she was sitting in a chair by the side of the bed.

Chapter Two

Meanwhile, in the illegal immigrants' detention centre, a few yards along the road from the hospital, a group of inmates were huddled together in deep discussion. The guard eyed the group uneasily. Unsure what action to take, he glanced nervously at his watch. In five minutes he would be off duty. Thankfully he turned his back on the group and walked towards the staff room to collect his coat from the locker room. A group of his colleagues were gathered together discussing the success of the local football team and their impending promotion to the Premier League. He joined in the discussion and quickly forgot his unease. However, the group of immigrants were still in deep discussion.

Sergie, a tall, dark-haired, bearded young man led the debate. He was angry and wanted to know why their plans had gone awry. Frankie, lightly built and of oriental appearance, tried to explain.

'It was all going as we planned. The patients were asleep and unlikely to wake. I had made sure of that.'

Sergie broke into Frankie's explanation.

'So why did it go wrong?'

Chang, another oriental man spoke up.

'We were ready to go, everything was in place and Frankie went down the ward to check everyone was sleeping. He went to check the drip that had been primed to explode and, as he shone his torch on the apparatus, the patient stirred and appeared to be wide awake. She wanted to know what he was doing. She called him a silly fool.'

Frankie interrupted with, 'I panicked and went to ask Sean what I should do.'

'You idiot!' shouted Sergie. 'Why didn't you go ahead and blow her up?'

Frankie continued. 'As I walked back to the nurses' station, the silly old bat shouted out that she needed help. The commotion disturbed some of the other patients and two nurses from F Ward came rushing in to investigate the disturbance. Seeing two friendly faces, the old lady said that she had pulled the tube from her leg. There was blood everywhere and she had tried to stem the flow by wrapping the sheet around her leg. It was impossible to go ahead with our plan to take over the hospital. Sean and his wife Colleen remade the bed and put the soiled sheets in the laundry basket. The rest of the terrorists disappeared before they were discovered. Staff Nurse wanted to know why the old lady had pulled the drip tube from her leg. The old lady, realising that there was no longer any immediate danger, said that she thought the hospital was being taken over by terrorists and wanted to save the other patients.'

'What a complete shambles,' Sergie said. 'The whole operation ruined because of your incompetence, Frankie.'

Abdullah, who came from Iran and was a handsome young man with a beard and shining brown eyes, had, up to now, remained silent. But now he interrupted with authority.

'We need the hospital as a base. Without it our operation will fail. It is in an ideal situation, so close to the harbour. I will pass the message round that the operation is delayed for two weeks whilst we decide how to proceed. For now, we must disperse. The night staff will soon be on duty and there will be no chance for those of you that are going to work at the hospital, to make your escape.'

Within minutes the group had gone their separate ways. The hospital workers found the escape route and disappeared into the night as silently as they had arrived at the centre. The other men made their way to the dormitories to settle down for the night.

Back in the staff quarters the night shift began their duties. Harry Chambers read the notes left by the day staff, picked up his torch and made his way to the dormitories. The night air was chilly and he pulled his collar up around his neck. It was dark and cloudy. He thought that someone moved across the compound, so he shone his torch but could see nothing. He must have been mistaken. Feeling threatened he quickened his steps. Satisfied that everything was in order he began his patrol of the perimeter fence. Three minutes earlier he would have come across the interlopers making their exit from the grounds but now everything seemed normal. He reached the main gate and exchanged a few words with Mickie Jones and Joe White, who were on night duty. He then continued round the perimeter. He entered the main building and proceeded to the staff room where two of his colleagues were making coffee.

'Everything okay, Harry?' said Bill Johnson, who would be the next guard to check the perimeter fences.

'All quiet and secure,' replied Harry. He then made his way over to the screens, which showed pictures from the security cameras, to make sure that everything was still in order. Satisfied with what he saw he joined his colleagues at the table. Bill produced a pack of cards and dealt them to his friends.

Chapter Three

Back at the hospital, AB had spent the day recovering from the operation and getting used to the daily routine. Soon the visitors would arrive and she looked forward to seeing her daughter and son-in-law. When they arrived they were amazed to see AB sitting by the side of the bed. The grandchildren had accompanied them and were anxious to know the gory details of the operation. Having satisfied them with details of what the operation had entailed, AB quietly told her daughter what had taken place after the operation. Sally looked quite alarmed but AB told her there was nothing to worry about, as she had most likely imagined the whole thing.

After the visitors left, everyone settled down for the night. The lights were dimmed and the night staff arrived for duty. AB felt apprehensive but when Frankie appeared with the drugs trolley she managed a smile. She accepted the painkillers but refused something to make her sleep. The hot chocolate was offered but again AB said, 'No thanks.' All around her the patients began to drift into sleep but AB remained wide awake. The endless to and fro of the staff, the clicking of the machinery and the banging of doors meant that AB wasn't going to get much sleep that night. However, she did drift in and out of sleep throughout the night but was relieved when the night staff went off duty and another day had dawned.

As the days went by, AB was soon making good progress and both doctor and physiotherapist were satisfied that the operation had been a success. She was quite mobile now, and challenged fellow patients to a race up the ward. It hadn't taken very long to get accustomed to the crutches but the white stockings were hardly a fashion statement. With each new day she began to look forward to the return home.

On the fourth day the physiotherapist said, 'You'll be going home tomorrow, but first you have to pass the stairs test.'

So it was off down the corridor to the nearest staircase and then a lesson on how to go up and down the stairs.

The physiotherapist said, 'Remember when going downstairs, its wounded knee first – down to hell – and when going up it's the good knee first – up to heaven.'

The task accomplished, the physiotherapist recommended to the doctor that AB should be discharged the next day. AB was over the moon!

The next day AB waited anxiously for the doctor's round to begin. She was unable to settle down to read and the morning dragged on. At last the doctor arrived and, having studied AB's chart, said that she could be discharged. As she had to wait for her son-in-law to come and fetch her, AB was moved to the waiting room to allow a new patient to occupy her bed. At last her son-in-law arrived and the staff nurse summoned a porter, with a wheelchair, to take AB to the car park.

As the car left the hospital grounds, AB felt like she had escaped from prison. She was filled with a feeling of relief. The journey was tiring but at last she was home and, satisfied that AB was able to look after herself, her son-in-law departed. It was going to be hard without any help but AB was determined that she would manage somehow. The first two weeks were very difficult and there were moments of frustration. Family and neighbours rallied round and gradually AB began to improve. As the weeks went by, she discarded the crutches in favour of two sticks. There were several highlights in her recovery: going on a bus to town, driving the car again and going for a swim, to name but a few. It took 12 weeks to get back into a normal routine but there was little that she was unable to tackle.

Chapter Four

Two days after the failed raid on the hospital, Abdullah took his usual escape route from the detention centre. He walked purposefully down the causeway without a backward glance. Within minutes a vehicle drew up alongside. A door was flung open and Abdullah climbed into the back of the car that then sped away from the dock area. The occupants of the car were all Iranians and were delighted to see Abdullah. They had been told that the planned operation had failed and offered their condolences. Abdullah asked if they knew when the next attempt would take place. The driver of the car, Sherriff, said that no decision had yet been made. The car sped along the A32 and headed towards the Meon Valley. Little more was said about the failed raid, although Sherriff said he was of the opinion they should not encourage other nationals to join the group, as they were a liability.

Soon they were in the open country and Sherriff turned off the main road into a single-track lane. There were a few houses along the lane and shortly they turned down a track that led to an old farmhouse. It was a fairly large building that was in need of renovation. There were several outbuildings, including stables.

Sherriff parked the car in one of the barns and the men climbed out of the car and made their way to the farmhouse. A few children were playing in the field and waved a welcome. As they entered the farmhouse a smell of cooking greeted them and the sound of women's laughter drifted from the kitchen.

Abdullah and Sherriff were both married with children but the other men were young and single. The children attended the local school and the families had been accepted into the community. No one had any idea what terrible deeds Abdullah and Sherriff were about to embark upon. Everyone sat round the table for a meal and the conversation was mainly about conditions in the detention camp.

After the meal Sherriff and Abdullah retired to a room at the back of the house that served as a study. Abdullah picked up the telephone and dialled a number. He asked when the operation was to go ahead and was surprised that the delay was going to be for six months. Apparently, the different factions couldn't agree and so time was needed to smooth out the problems. Sherriff was furious!

'I told you we shouldn't encourage other nationals to take part,' he said. 'Why we don't strike out on our own, I don't know?'

'It seems a long while to wait,' Abdullah agreed, 'and the men will get restless.'

Meanwhile the young men had left the farmhouse and made their way to the local pub where they had been accepted as regular customers. One of the men ordered drinks and they all gathered round the dartboard and began to play.

'How's it going up on the farm?' asked one old timer called Bert. 'Are you settling in okay?'

One of the men answered, choosing his words very carefully. 'Couldn't be better,' he said. 'We're hoping to get some sheep soon.

The old timer said, 'If you need any advice, I'm your man. Not much I don't know about sheep.'

On the way back to the farmhouse, the men were in high spirits. Their stay in the village could prove to be quite enjoyable.

When they reached Woodville Farm, Sherriff broke the news of the setback to the men. He was surprised at their reaction to the six-month delay. When they told him of their decision to take part in the village activities he agreed that it was a good idea. Sherriff drove Abdullah back to the detention centre around midnight. He left Abdullah by the entrance to the escape route. Abdullah scaled the wall and, checking that the guard was not in view, climbed down into the compound then made his way to his dormitory. Everything was quiet and he settled down for the night.

In the morning, everyone wanted to know what was going to happen so, when the guards changed over at 8.30 am, Abdullah called a meeting. He explained the six-month delay. Of course the men were disappointed. They had hoped to be free in a few days. Morale was low and Abdullah knew that he must do something to lift the spirits of those awaiting deportation.

Chapter Five

Rob Petrie left his apartment in Gunwharf Quays at 7.20 am and walked in the direction of Portsmouth Harbour Station. He glanced at his watch and quickened his pace. The train to London was timed to leave at 7.45 am and he didn't want to miss it. As he approached the bus station two buses pulled into the terminus and people hurriedly dismounted. Beryl and Mary Jones headed for the Gosport Ferry en route to the hospital.

Mary said, 'No need to rush, we've plenty of time.'

Beryl agreed and remarked that it was going to be a lovely day. The sea was calm and the weather set fair.

A small car pulled up in front of the station. Two men got out and quickly walked away. They headed off towards Gunwharf Quays to mingle with the shoppers. No words passed between them.

Rob thought that it was an odd place to leave a car unattended. They'd probably get a parking ticket or maybe they'd be clamped. He smiled and walked on his way.

Mary and Beryl bought return ferry tickets from the machine then started to walk across the road to watch for its arrival. It was just another ordinary day. The Warrior made a perfect picture on this fine day but the hurrying crowds paid little attention to its beauty.

Suddenly, without warning, there was a mighty explosion. The car in front of the station had disintegrated along with the station entrance. A thick dust seemed to fill the air and the cries of the injured echoed all around. Rob Petrie was no more! He had been killed outright. Across the road, Mary looked in horror at the scene. She turned to speak to Beryl who lay injured on the pavement having been struck by flying debris from the explosion. Beryl was losing quite a lot of blood and Mary knelt by her side to comfort her daughter.

The initial panic was over and several people had used their mobile phones to phone the emergency services. A train had just pulled into the station and the passengers were shepherded back onto it, despite angry protests from those who were unaware of the disaster that had taken place. The train then swiftly pulled out of the station.

Surprisingly there was little damage to the arrival and departure bays, although there was concern that the front of the station might collapse completely. Also the café and the waiting room had been completely demolished. It had quickly been decided that all trains would now terminate at Southsea.

A dishevelled Mrs Hardcastle emerged from the ladies toilet completely covered in dust but otherwise uninjured. She could not believe the scene that met her eyes. How fortunate she had been not to be killed!

Emergency teams swiftly went to work and gradually the injured were despatched to hospital. Mary accompanied her daughter Beryl to QA Hospital but knew that she was unlikely to survive.

The local radio stations were quickly at the scene and a news bulletin was broadcast giving an account of the devastation. There was an air of disbelief among the local population. How could this happen in such a secure area?

Considering the number of people in the vicinity, the casualties were few, 20 dead and 50 injured, but many of those injuries were light, although six remained in intensive care.

Liz Petrie had heard the explosion and had listened to the news bulletin. She left home immediately and hurried to the station. Liz had tried to reach Rob on his mobile telephone but was unable to get a reply. No one was able to tell her what had happened to Rob. The casualties had all been taken to QA Hospital so Liz made her way there.

The two men from the car that exploded had walked to Gunwharf Quays car park where Ali was waiting for them at the lower level. They quickly climbed into the vehicle and Ali drove to the Cascades car park. Ali parked and the men made for the escalator. They descended to the food floor and purchased coffee and Danish pastries. There was a buzz of conversation as the news had filtered through to the busy shopping centre. One of the men leaned across to the next table and asked if they knew who had planted the bomb.

'The general opinion is that it's the work of the IRA,' said one man.

Once they had finished their snack, the three men made their way to the lift and, on reaching the car park, walked casually to their car.

They drove out of Portsmouth on the Eastern Road, heading for the A3M.

Abdullah turned to Sherriff and said, 'A job well done, I think you will agree.'

Sherriff nodded. 'The men should be happy with our action and it will help to lessen their disappointment over the delay.'

The police were unable to get a description of the two men in the car. The only man who saw them clearly was dead!

Chapter Six

Shaun and Colleen McInness left the hospital by car in the early hours of the morning and drove towards the M27. They were heading for North Wales and the Holyhead Ferry. Shaun had decided that the time had come to report back to IRA headquarters on the situation so far. He was unhappy with the way things were going and would have liked more say in planned operations. He hoped to get increased backing to give him a more important role in the future.

He left the M27 motorway and turned onto the M3, heading north. The rain was ceaseless and their spirits sank to an all-time low. The journey seemed long and tedious. When they reached the M6 they stopped for a break at the Stafford Service Area but did not linger for long as Shaun was impatient to continue the journey. After travelling for another hour they eventually reached the A55 and had soon crossed the border into North Wales. They decided to stop in Conwy where they ate the sandwiches and drank the water that they had purchased at the Stafford Service Area. After the welcome break they journeyed on to Caernarfon and the Celtic Royal Hotel. The journey had taken them four hours. They checked into the hotel in the name of Condon and then took the lift to their room.

At 8.00 pm they went down to the restaurant and spent a relaxing two hours discussing hospital procedures never once mentioning the purpose of their visit to Ireland the

they would be successful. Leaving Kathleen in the kitchen, Colleen joined the girls in their bedroom and Kathleen was delighted to hear sounds of laughter coming from upstairs. She smiled contently but had she heard the conversation that was taking place, at The Castle Arms, between the boys she would have been devastated.

Dan left the office early and made his way straight home expecting to see Sean and Colleen and he was disappointed that Sean had gone off with the boys. Kathleen broke the news that the Callaghan brothers were also at The Castle Arms. He felt uneasy and hoped his suspicions were unjustified.

Chapter Seven

Back in Britain, AB looked up from the *Daily Telegraph* general knowledge crossword as a news bulletin flashed up on the television. She listened, with utter disbelief, as the details of the bomb attack in Portsmouth were announced. Suddenly she felt convinced that there had been an attempt on her life at the hospital and that a terror attack had been planned. A moment of panic swiftly passed. It was hardly likely that the terrorists would try to trace her now. After all, at the time, she had hinted that she had been hallucinating. No point informing the police, they too would think that she was mad. She did wonder where the perpetrators had disappeared to after they left the car. Perhaps they had gone to the Asylum Detention Centre. AB put the *Telegraph* to one side and got ready to go into Waterlooville. She needed to go to the bank and the Post Office. Leaving the bungalow, she walked to the car and got into the driver's seat. It took some time to get the car started as it was temperamental when starting from cold. Breathing a sigh of relief, she drove away. As AB turned into the main road she had an uneasy feeling that she was being followed. Looking into her mirror she could see a black car close on her tail. It occurred to AB that the black car had followed her before. Was this just a coincidence? She decided to test her suspicion and took a turning to the left. Then, at the next roundabout, she went right and headed back towards her home. The black car was still on her tail. Feeling nervous, she decided to head to town once more. As she reached the large car park she again turned off to the left. AB found a parking space and walked off to get a ticket. The black car was now nowhere to be seen. Relieved, AB made her way to the bank. She began to think that she had been mistaken and that perhaps it was just a coincidence.

The black car drove towards the Meon Valley. The driver turned to speak to his passenger.

'I think she knows we were following her,' he said.

'Yes, I think you're right,' said the passenger. 'We best get further instructions.'

At Woodville Farm everyone was in high spirits. It was now operating as a going concern and the families had been accepted into the community. Ali now had a regular girlfriend. Maggie Petersen was a farmer's daughter and adored Ali. Her parents thought that Ali was a likeable lad but Greg Petersen did have his reservations. He had hoped that Maggie would marry an Englishman and he did feel slightly uneasy about his daughter's relationship with this foreign lad.

Abdul was also dating Sarah, another of the village girls, but she had a wide circle of friends and she didn't look on her relationship with Abdul as a permanent arrangement. However, it was fun while it lasted. The foursome was in the darts team and visited various public houses in the area to take part in matches. When they were alone, the girls would discuss their relationships with the two foreigners. Sarah had enjoyed protected sex with Abdul but she wasn't in love with him. Maggie said that she wouldn't have sex unless she was madly in love and wanted to get married. Sarah laughed at this and told Maggie to have some fun. Secretly, she thought that Ali might not have the same views as Maggie and that he would get his sex life elsewhere.

Lee Kuan and Chang Li arrived back at Woodville Farm and quickly found Sherriff. They told him that AB had probably realised she was being followed. Sherriff was angry and hoped that it wouldn't jeopardise their plans. Abdullah would be at the farm in the evening and he would ask him what action they should take.

When Abdullah arrived later in the day, he went straight to the office. Sherriff quickly joined him there and told him the latest news. Abdullah asked Sherriff what he thought AB would do. Sherriff said that he thought it unlikely that she would go to the police and no one was going to believe her anyway. Abdullah had received a text message from Pakistan. Apparently, some of the other groups had complained that they weren't being informed of planned operations. The message went on to tell Abdullah to keep everyone aware of future plans. It continued by saying that a summit meeting would take place shortly, to discuss the major action that had been postponed. Probably the meeting would take place in Spain.

Chapter Eight

Portsmouth Football Club was playing Arsenal at Fratton Park and, before the match took place, a cheerful crowd of home supporters filled the roads around the ground. In the midst of the crowd were a dozen men looking for a fight. These men were not supporters but organised troublemakers looking for an opportunity to cause a riot. Tubby Westward and Jimmy Cook grinned at each other.

'There is going to be a summit meeting soon,' said Tubby. 'Do you want to go Jim?'

'Are you going?' asked Jim.

'Yeah, I can't wait to get in on the action,' said Tubby.

'Okay, count me in,' said Jim.

Suddenly there was a commotion in front of them. Fists were flying and people screaming. Parents desperately tried to remove their children to a place of safety. The police began to disperse the crowd and made a few arrests but the 12 men melted into the background. Ambulances took the injured to QA Hospital. The police escorted the football supporters to the ground and the match went ahead after a 30-minute delay.

There was no more trouble during the match and when the final whistle blew, the visiting side's supporters were allowed out of the ground first. Jim and Tubby made their way to the nearest public house and when they finally headed home they were very drunk.

Chapter Nine

Two young men left Kabul, in Afghanistan, and travelled towards the border with Pakistan. They were on their way to receive instruction, in their religion, from Islamic elders. They had been reluctant to say goodbye to their families but were looking forward to meeting up with new friends. The boys were typical teenagers, keen for adventure and full of fun. At the border crossing they entered Pakistan without any problems and travelled on to the village of Damadola where they quickly found the house they were seeking. It had been arranged that they would stay overnight at this house and that the following morning a vehicle would collect them in order that they should continue their journey to a boarding school near Peshawar. They received a warm welcome at the village house and looked forward to the next day.

Back in Kabul, two mothers had been sad to see their sons depart and hoped that they would soon return home.

In the morning, the boys left the village for their journey to Peshawar. On arriving at the school, they were amazed to see so many young boys and quickly made friends. However, they were slightly dismayed when they were summoned to a room where they would begin their indoctrination. There was no room for time wasting and learning the Koran, line by line, was strictly adhered to but it was a relief when they were able to leave the room and join their new friends in the gymnasium. The regime in this part of the school was very strict and there was little time for socialising.

After they had been at the school for two weeks they were summoned to the head's office. They were told to wait outside the office until called and eventually the first boy entered the head's room. This lad was told that he had been specially chosen to carry out the work of Allah and that, if he did as directed, he would become a martyr and his family would be doubly blessed! He felt very proud that he had been chosen for this task and began to wonder what he would have to do. He was ordered to study hard during his stay at the school and make sure he learned all he could. When he left the room, his friend was summoned and given the same information.

At the end of that week the boys were called to the laboratory and joined a group of 20 boys studying various methods of making bombs. They all thought it was great fun. At the same time, they learned how to place car bombs and where to leave bombs in strategic places. It had not dawned on the two boys that they would take part in this kind of activity.

During the following week, they were told how they could become martyrs by blowing themselves up and, if they were to become suicide bombers, they would bring great honour to their families. All they had learned overawed the 20 boys but it is doubtful whether, at this stage, any of them envisaged that they would be taking part in these activities. In the main school building that was situated some distance away, there was no evidence that any untoward activity was taking place. Like any other boarding school, the children were being taught general subjects and, although the discipline was fairly rigid, no one would suspect that across the playing field, in a building hidden from view, boys were being trained in warfare. The school was highly thought of by the local population and they were completely ignorant of the indoctrination classes for selected boys, who were mainly from foreign lands.

Chapter Ten

The Prime Minister opened the door to his office in the House of Commons and found his deputy awaiting his arrival.

The Prime Minister said, 'I understand that MI5 are asking for a special meeting.'

'ASAP,' replied his deputy.

'Well, let's fix it for tomorrow morning before 11.00 am,' said the Prime Minister. 'Any idea what it is all about?'

'None at all,' replied his deputy.

After discussing the business for the day, the two men left the office and walked along the corridor towards the central lobby and then on to the Commons chamber.

A short way away from the Houses of Parliament, on the top floor of an office block, two men and a woman were locked into deep discussion.

Rosie Page said that she had received intelligence from a reliable source that a meeting was to take place, in Spain, of various terrorist organisations from several nations and it was thought that a major operation was, no doubt, being planned. Roger Johnson said that he had received notification from an agent in Iraq that representatives from many Arab countries were to hold a summit meeting, in

31

Morocco, prior to the meeting in Spain. James King said that he was sure that something of great importance was about to happen and he was concerned that only Arabs had been invited to take part.

'We need permission from the Prime Minister to ascertain what is on the agenda for this meeting,' he said.

The next day, the Prime Minister and his deputy made their way, through the rain, to the offices of MI5. In the hurrying crowds, they went unnoticed and entered the MI5 building around 9.30 am. Glad to be out of the rain, they took the lift to the top of the building and made their way to the office of Rosie Page. Rosie, Roger and James were awaiting the two men, having been buzzed by reception that they were on their way. Rosie lifted the internal phone and ordered coffee and biscuits for five. When the Prime Minister and his deputy arrived at Rosie's office, she quickly explained the purpose of the meeting and her concerns that something big was being planned. The PM asked if anything more had come through from intelligence but she said that she had given him all the up to date information.

'Has there been any further progress in finding the Portsmouth bombers?' the PM asked.

'No, I'm afraid not,' said Rosie. 'They seem to have disappeared without leaving any clues.'

The Deputy PM was furious.

'What do we pay you for?' he said.

James replied, 'I say, that's a bit unfair. We have been pulling out all the stops and Roger has agents working all out to find the perpetrators.'

There was an uncomfortable silence and the PM tried his best to get the conversation back on track. Anxiously glancing at his watch, he asked if there was anything more that they wished to discuss. Rosie said that she would keep him informed as and when more news came to hand. With that, the PM and his deputy left the room. The deputy was still ranting about incompetence but the PM rounded on him saying that it was a difficult and dangerous job that our agents do. They walked back to the House of Commons, through the continuing rain, in silence. The deputy was anxious to call a cabinet meeting but the PM said it was not necessary at this stage, repeating that it was a difficult and dangerous job that our agents do. Still mumbling to himself, the Deputy left the Prime Minister's office without making further comment but felt annoyed that the Cabinet were not to be informed.

When the deputy left his office, the Prime Minister picked up the telephone and was soon speaking to the Foreign Secretary.

'Meet me at Number Ten around 3.00 pm. I've something I wish to discuss with you in private,' he said.

Chapter Eleven

The President of Russia was talking to his ambassador in the United States. The conversation went like this:

'I'm very concerned about the continued terrorist attacks around the world and, of course, the activity in Kazakhstan. We must persuade the Americans and British to withdraw their troops from Iraq. I see this as the only way to put the brakes on the escalating number of bomb attacks that are occurring.'

The ambassador replied, 'I will do my best to set up a summit meeting between Russia, America and Britain but it won't be easy as they are adamant that their troops should stay in Iraq.'

The Russian President ended the phone call having left the matter in the hands of his ambassador.

In a Marrakech hotel, there was a buzz of activity as staff prepared for a meeting of Arabs from various countries. The hotel was fully booked for the next two weeks and the booking included use of all the leisure activities, the conference hall and the restaurants. Those attending this meeting were fanatical Muslims who wished to spread their religion across the world and were prepared to use any method to annihilate infidels. These men were not representing the majority of Muslims but they had strong religious beliefs that left them blinkered and unable to accept that other people had the right to freedom of choice. Some of these men were very wealthy and prepared to fund terrorist activities.

Sheikh Hassan had arranged the meeting in Marrakech. He was a wealthy and influential Arab and according to British intelligence, he was a very dangerous individual, prepared to pay large sums of money to those willing to support his plans.

To the many tourists in the area, the significance of so many Arabs entering the hotel went unnoticed. This was, after all, an Arab country.

In a nearby restaurant, four men drinking coffee in the far corner were in deep discussion. These men were in Marrakech for a specific purpose. Two came from America and the other two men came from Britain. All four men were secret agents and hoped to attend the summit meeting to ascertain what the Arabs were planning. They had false identities and papers but were aware of the dangers of their mission.

The first meeting of the Arabs was due to take place the next day in the conference hall. Security was very tight and special passes had been issued to those summoned to attend the meeting. The secret agents had managed to befriend an Iranian Arab, who was open to bribery, and for the right price he guaranteed to provide the agents with four passes. As the agents ordered more coffee, the Iranian joined them at their table and, once the money had been paid, the forged passes were handed over. They couldn't believe it had been that easy! The Iranian disappeared into the crowds of tourists outside the restaurant.

Sheikh Hassan addressed the meeting the next day. He spoke proudly of the achievements of the Muslim cause and the hope of achieving a Muslim world and ridding nations of infidels. He described the task ahead as a mammoth one and said that many sacrifices would have to be made. Those who gave their lives would become martyrs and their

35

families would be taken care of. They would want for nothing. He went on to say that it was intended, with the help of terrorists groups from other countries, to take control of Britain and America, starting with the invasion of Britain. He regretted that there had been one failed attempt but he was confident the next attempt would be successful.

'We have reliable people, in strategic places, and they will ensure that the terrorists from various organisations around the world will be organised to create diversions from the main operation.'

At question time, the main concerns were that the various organisations had different agendas but Hassan assured the meeting that this matter would be addressed, and hopefully resolved, at the meeting that was to take place in Spain.

Further meetings took place during the next two weeks and it was clear Hassan was confident that, by the end of the two weeks, he would have the support of his Arab colleagues.

The secret agents had attended all the meetings and, dressed as Arabs, had gone undetected. Coded messages were sent to Britain and America with the relevant details of the plans for the months ahead.

When Rosie Page received the message she immediately telephoned the Prime Minister, who subsequently got in touch with the President of the United States. Security forces, in both countries, were immediately put on red alert. However, it was not known when the attacks were to take place. Delegates from various interested terrorist groups had received invitations to attend a meeting in the Costa del Sol where they could state their aims and elaborate on any actions they intended taking. The delegates arriving for this meeting were certainly a mixed group of individuals. Abdullah and Sherriff had received their invitations, as had Tubby and Jim, the football supporters. Invitations had also been sent to the IRA, ETA (the Basque Separatists), Iraqi supporters of Saddam, Iranians, various Russian groups and delegates from Pakistan, Afghanistan, Libya, Egypt, Zimbabwe and many other countries.

The hotel for the meeting had been selected by Sheikh Hassan, who had paid a substantial deposit and was to pay for all expenses at the end of the week's stay. The meeting was billed as a meeting for those interested in scientific research. It was situated near a golf course and many of those arriving for the meeting had come equipped with their golf clubs.

It was difficult to see what any of these groups had in common and how they could be used to further the Muslim extremists' cause. It would take the skill of Hassan to convince the diverse groups that their cooperation would be essential for the overall plan. Hassan arranged minor meetings, for each group, to ascertain how they wished to further their cause and to deal with any complaints that they had.

On the final day, Hassan addressed a meeting of all the delegates. He said that the starting point for the ongoing campaign was to be a concerted attack on British and American targets and that any assistance the individual groups could give would be of considerable help. The aim was to demoralise the British and Americans and to bring them to their knees, making it easier for the various groups to negotiate terms for monetary aid for their campaigns. All British and American targets around the world would be liable to be attacked. There was a buzz of excitement around the conference hall and the four special agents were astonished at the unanimous support Hassan was given and, when the meeting came to a close, Hassan received a standing ovation.

On the golf course, later that day, the agents all agreed that Hassan was a clever man who had completely fooled the delegates as to the Arabs' reasons for their commitment to this campaign. The agents had already sent coded messages to their head offices warning of the dangers. When they finally reached the bar, the main topic of conversation was Hassan.

Tubby and Jim stood at the bar and were, perhaps, alone in wondering what was in this campaign for them! After all, what they wanted in life was to enjoy a good drink and to have a punch-up. Their main aim was to rouse rival gangs to violence and then stand back and have a good laugh at the consequences.

Chapter Twelve

In Hampshire, Woodville Farm was now an established business in the Meon Valley. The labour force had been increased and the new workers were welcomed in the village. Ali and Maggie were still good friends and Ali spent most of his leisure hours with Maggie and her family. To his annoyance, Maggie's father had found out very little about Ali's family. Ali seemed reluctant to talk about his early life and this worried Maggie's parents. After all, it could be that they would not agree to Ali getting married to Maggie.

Greg Petersen and his wife Sue discussed the matter with Maggie but the discussion ended in a blazing row and Maggie flounced out of the farmhouse. She knew her parents were right but when she had asked Ali about his family he had become very angry and wouldn't answer her questions, so she had avoided the subject ever since. Head over heels in love with Ali, Maggie was concerned that he seemed reluctant to discuss his future plans. Her friend Sarah was not very helpful either. Sarah had said that Ali would get fed up with the relationship if Maggie didn't have sexual intercourse with him soon. Maggie began to believe her friend, as Ali had tried to take their relationship further on two occasions recently. Firstly, he had slid his hand inside her blouse and caressed her breasts pressing his body firmly against her. She had been overwhelmed by his actions but knew it would be wrong to allow him to go further and had pulled away from Ali. Then, one evening, in the local pub, Ali bought drinks for the four friends. Ali, Abdul and Maggie always had non-alcoholic drinks but Sarah drank beer. That night Ali decided to buy beer for Maggie. At first, Maggie objected but she decided that she quite enjoyed the taste of beer. As the evening wore on, she had consumed quite a few beers. They left the pub in a jolly mood and Maggie was quite drunk. Abdul and Sarah went and sat in Abdul's car and Ali called goodnight to them both, as he and Maggie walked off in the direction of Elmwood farm. Ali started to kiss Maggie and unfastened her blouse but, despite the fact that she had drunk too much beer, she was aware that Ali was about to rob her of her virginity. She broke away and ran falteringly towards home. Ali was furious! He left her to find her own way home and he turned to walk in the direction of Woodville Farm.

Greg Petersen looked up from his book as his daughter arrived home and he was furious at the state that Maggie was in. She hadn't fastened her blouse and was swaying from side to side. For the first time that he could remember he lost his temper.

'Go to bed!' he yelled, I'll speak to you in the morning.'

However, Maggie was in no fit state to speak to anyone the following day.

Having finished helping with the milking, Greg Petersen strode across the top field, climbed over the stile into the lane and walked purposely in the direction of Woodville Farm where Ali worked. It was a cold, crisp, morning but Greg didn't feel the cold. He was fired up with rage. There were men working in the field and they gave him a friendly wave but he took no notice. As he turned into the long driveway of the farm, a message was sent from the security officer, manning the cameras, to Abdullah that a visitor was approaching the farmhouse. Abdullah left the farmhouse and walked down the drive. On his way to meet Greg, he called to Sherriff to be on his guard.

As Greg drew near to Abdullah, he called out, 'Where can I find Ali?'

Abdullah thought quickly and answered, 'He's out with the delivery van. Can I help you?'

Greg felt frustrated. He decided to discuss his concerns with Abdullah and he asked him if he could talk to him about Ali. Abdullah invited him to the farmhouse and, passing through the kitchen, told one of the girls to bring some coffee. Greg noted the opulence of Abdullah's office and quickly realised that the farm must be a thriving business. As they sat drinking tea, Greg explained the reason for his visit and then went on to say that he hoped that Ali's feelings for Maggie were genuine and that he intended to ask her to marry him in due course. He also expressed his dismay with regard to the lack of information concerning Ali's family. Abdullah explained that Ali's family lived in Iran and that he was promised to a Pakistani girl. He would get in touch with them to get their views. Greg began to feel uneasy. He left the farmhouse and hurried back along the drive. His mind was in turmoil as he turned into the lane and he regretted that he was unable to talk to Ali.

Waiting until Greg had departed, Abdullah called Sherriff to his office. He told him about Greg's anger and said he was unclear what action he ought to take. He knew that if he sent Ali home it could jeopardise the relationship between the villagers and the farm workers but there had to be a solution fairly quickly. Sherriff suggested that they could use Ali as a bomber but Abdullah said that this could mean that the police investigation that followed the bombing could trace Ali back to the farm.

Abdullah decided that it would be best if Ali and Maggie became engaged and so he called Ali to his office to discuss a course of action. It was agreed that Ali should apologise to Greg and ask if he could marry Maggie.

When Greg arrived back at his farm he found that Maggie had gone out with Sarah. Greg and Sue discussed his meeting with Abdullah and they agreed to work together to end Maggie's association with Ali. When Ali arrived at their farm the next day and asked if he could marry Maggie, they were dumbfounded. Ali assured them that he had no intention of going back home for an arranged marriage and that he was very much in love with Maggie. He said that Abdullah had talked to Ali's father who had agreed that he should marry Maggie in England.

Ali booked a meal at a local restaurant for the following day and went off to buy an engagement ring for Maggie. When Maggie arrived home, she had fully recovered her composure and was surprised that nothing was said about her behaviour the previous day. Ali called early the next morning to apologise to Maggie and to invite her to have dinner with him that evening. She was overwhelmed with love for Ali and accepted his invitation.

As they waited for their coffee, after an excellent meal, Ali produced the ring and asked for her hand in marriage. She was thrilled but said that she must ask her parents for their agreement. Ali told her that he already had her father's permission. She could hardly believe him but she put the ring on her finger and was so happy. The meal over, they hastened to the Petersen's farm to inform Greg and Sue of the engagement and to discuss arrangements for the party. Greg and Sue still had reservations about the future happiness of their daughter and Greg had a premonition that he would regret his decision to give the couple his blessing. However, they seemed blissfully happy and, as the news spread through the village, everyone seemed delighted.

Sarah was surprised that Maggie had decided to marry Ali and said that she had no intention of marrying Abdul. She was far too busy enjoying her freedom but she hoped that Maggie would be very happy.

As the invitations to the engagement party went out to Greg and Sue's relations and friends, many of them asked Greg if he was happy about a mixed marriage. He was warned that some Muslims had very strong religious beliefs and that there could be trouble ahead. Greg became uneasy about Ali's parents but Abdullah had assured him that they had given their consent to the marriage, so he pushed his doubts to the back of his mind. When the replies to the invitations were received, there were a few polite letters of apology regretting inability to attend the celebrations but in the main Greg and Maggie's friends and relations were happy to attend. Greg thought that some of those apologising for not being able to attend were probably racially motivated and he was saddened by their attitude.

Ali's friends from Woodville Farm came along. Abdullah arrived at the party with Sherriff. He said that he had a proposition to put to the young couple. He took Ali and Maggie to one side and said that there was a vacancy, for a farm hand, at another of his properties in Suffolk, and that there was a two-bedroom cottage vacant on the site that would be suitable for Maggie and Ali, if they were interested, but they would have to marry before moving to the cottage. Of course, they were delighted but when Greg heard the news he was crestfallen. He had hoped that they would have a long engagement and that eventually they would decide that they weren't in love. Abdullah said that the offer to accept the job would be left open for three months but Ali and Maggie were so excited that they were already making plans for the wedding. Ali was happy to get married in a Christian church and said that they would have a Muslim ceremony in Iran at a later date.

The wedding took place, two months later, in the village church. It was well attended, despite the short notice, but Ali's parents were unable to come from Iran for the ceremony. Sarah was bridesmaid and Abdul was best man. Maggie looked radiant. She wore her mother's wedding dress that had been altered to fit her. Greg's heart missed a beat when he saw how beautiful she looked.

It had been arranged for Maggie and Ali to spend their honeymoon in the cottage and Ali would start work on the new farm after two weeks. The cottage had been redecorated before they moved in and so they spent the two weeks getting to know the neighbourhood. Ali soon sought out Assam, who managed the farm, and told Maggie that he was very happy to work for his new boss.

Greg and Sue missed Maggie and eagerly awaited her telephone calls but it was impossible to leave the farm to visit Maggie as there was too much work for them to do, but they hoped to make the journey later in the year.

Chapter Thirteen

For AB life had returned to normal. She was unaware that anyone was following her now and began to think that all danger had passed. Although bombs had exploded in several countries around the world and people had been killed or injured, there had not been any attacks on the scale of the twin towers. Life in London had settled down after the attacks there and people were carrying on their lives once more. The tourists had returned and the red alert had been withdrawn.

As the weeks, then months, went by people worried more about the bad weather than the terrorists. There was more than the average rainfall and gale force winds occurred in most parts of Britain. Several towns were flooded and people were made homeless. The scenes of devastation were heartbreaking. However, MI5 were still busy following up leads and Rosie Page, Roger and James were feeding information to the police concerning suspected terrorist activity in this country. Some arrests had been made but Rosie was convinced that there were other terrorist cells still operating. She had received a disturbing telephone call from Agent Charles concerning the training of a terrorist group in the New Forest and upon investigation, several arrests had taken place.

Overnight the Prime Minister and his deputy had resigned and excitement gripped the country. Would there be an election? However, the party chose a new leader and deputy and life continued as normal. There was no withdrawal of troops from Iraq and no election.

Rosie Page picked up her internal telephone and asked Roger if he and James could come to her office. When they arrived she dismissed her secretary and said that she was not to be disturbed. James asked what the problem was and she replied that she intended, in the light of what she considered was an escalation of terrorist activity in the country, to ask the Prime Minister to meet them as soon as possible. Roger was of the opinion that the New Forest episode was an isolated affair but James and Rosy were convinced, from agent reports, that other groups existed. Rosie picked up the telephone and dialled the Prime Minister's number. When she suggested that they should meet, he agreed that they had some important issues to discuss and, in view of the urgency, he would cancel his engagements for the next day and he and the Deputy Prime Minister would come to Rosie's office.

When the Prime Minister and his Deputy reached Rosie's office the next day, they both expressed their concern when Rosie said that she was unaware just how many of the terrorists' training groups existed. Rosie went on to say that intelligence had reported that Sheikh Hassan, and his entourage, were on the move and that other Muslim extremists were making arrangements to travel. However, the number involved was small and it could be that this was just a social gathering of his Muslim friends. The Deputy Prime Minister said that they must keep watching this situation, as something big could be planned in the near future. He went on to say that he thought the red alert should be reintroduced. Everyone agreed and with this, the Prime Minister and his deputy returned to Parliament.

Meanwhile, Sheikh Hassan summoned his aide to his office and expressed his dismay at the lack of support they were now receiving.

'We seem to be losing some of the extremists from around the world. With the peace initiative in Northern Ireland, the activities of the IRA have subsided and there are other signs of trouble spots in the world becoming peaceful once more,' he said.

Hassan's aide reluctantly agreed. Hassan asked him to arrange a meeting of extremist Muslims for the coming week.

'We will go to a coastal resort in order to make this look like an annual social gathering,' he said.

A hotel was booked in Dubai and those joining Hassan were expected to pay their own expenses. Several events were arranged and to the onlooker this was just an organised social occasion that gave no cause for concern.

Also visiting Dubai at this time were the four special agents: Charles, Freddie, Oscar and Peter. They mingled with the tourists and spent time on the beach and also lounging round the hotel pool, hoping to pick up some information concerning the Arab social event. There seemed little to concern them as they relaxed in the sunshine. However, as they ate a meal in the dining room that evening, they heard someone on the next table mention a British hospital. Oscar and Peter raised their eyebrows and strained to listen to the conversation but they could only make out a few phrases. The words private and hospitals were repeated several times but, although Oscar and Peter thought there was going to be an attack in Britain and it involved a hospital, it could have been anywhere in the British Isles. There was no further information during the meal. The agents decided to pass on the small amount of information that they had already gathered.

Sheikh Hassan outlined his plan to a select number of friends and said that he hoped he could rely on their support.

'Also,' he said, 'we must act quickly as we have less reliable support now. With the riots in Pakistan, it's probable that we will be unable to receive help from that quarter but I emphasise that we must act quickly or there will be no hope of success.'

He received unanimous support from those present and set a date for the following month.

At dinner that night, Agent Charles heard a date mentioned. It was 21st March. In discussion with his fellow agents, they agreed that this was most likely the date of a big attack on the British Isles. That evening he passed on the news to Rosie in London, and she informed the Prime Minister. They had just one month to put in the necessary arrangements for tight security around the hospitals of Britain. It was agreed that some army units would be recalled from overseas to make up the shortfall in home defence forces. Troop movements would be carried out secretly as far as possible. Reserve troops would also be called up to assist and the police and fire service would get top-secret information. A special meeting of the Cabinet was called and they were informed of the major alert.

Chapter Fourteen

AB now had a problem with her right knee and was finding it difficult to walk. After seeing the consultant, it was arranged that she should have a right knee replacement. Of course, she was apprehensive but in the spring AB entered the hospital for the operation.

Since her last visit to the hospital, there had been some alterations and redecoration of the wards. There was a more welcoming atmosphere and no sign of any of the staff that had been on her ward when she was last there. AB was in hospital for four days and thankfully, returned home without any unusual occurrences. It was six months before she began to drive again, so she spent most of the time at home. As the days passed, her experience during her first visit to the hospital faded into the distance and she was able to relax.

However, when her granddaughter came to see her one day she was very excited about her new boyfriend and said that he was really very nice. Emma had, at last, passed her driving test and had bought a car. She said that she had been to the Meon Valley and called in to a well-known country pub for a meal. She was surprised that there were several African and Asian young men having food in the restaurant. Apparently, they were working on a farm nearby.

Emma said, 'I think they must be Muslims as they weren't drinking alcohol. It seemed so strange seeing so many foreigners working out there but they were all very friendly.'

Memories flooded back to AB but she dismissed her thoughts quickly and put her concerns down to her overactive imagination. Emma began to visit the Meon Valley more often and enjoyed the social atmosphere in the country pub. One of the lads talked of the work on the farm and said that the owner had recently employed more staff because of the increased amount of work. When AB heard this she began to be concerned. How could this farmer need so many employees when others in the Meon Valley were finding it hard to make a profit?

Feeling that she had to prevent a disaster occurring, AB decided it was time to go to the police with her suspicions. As she walked into the police station, she knew that it was likely she would be dismissed as a crackpot but she was determined to do her best to convince them that they should, at least investigate the farm in the Meon Valley. The young police lady behind the desk looked up as AB approached her and smiled when she asked AB how she could help. AB hesitated for a moment then asked to see someone in authority. But it wasn't going to be that easy. The smile disappeared from the young police lady's face and she demanded to know what AB's problem was as she could probably help. AB persevered saying it was information concerning terrorists. The police lady tried to hide her amusement. She had decided that, as this woman was in her 70s she was probably confused and when a young detective entered the room, she took him to one side and asked if he could deal with AB's problem. He asked AB to follow him to an interview room. AB was not expecting to get any action from this young man but was glad to be able to discuss her fears with someone at last. The detective made a note of her name and address and listened to her story. When AB finally finished, he thanked her for coming and promised to look into the matter.

As AB left the police station, she could hear them laughing and realised that they didn't believe her story. The young detective asked the police lady to get in touch with Social Services and see if they had anything on this old lady and it was arranged that someone from Social Services would visit AB to see if she needed help. When AB arrived home she turned on the radio to listen to the news. She was startled to hear that the Prime Minister had made a statement to say that there would be no immediate withdrawal of troops from Iraq or Afghanistan. Also listening to that broadcast was Rosie Page and she was dumbfounded, particularly as the country was on red alert.

'What on earth was he playing at?' she wondered.

In the police canteen, the young detective was telling AB's story to his colleagues and not everyone was laughing. PC Everett decided to drive out to the Meon Valley, when he was off duty, to take a look. He parked on the hill opposite Woodville Farm and watched for any unusual signs of activity. He saw nothing unusual for some time and had almost given up. He turned his attention to the farm buildings. A door opened and a man came out of the farmhouse and walked towards a large outbuilding. PC Everett couldn't believe his eyes. He recognised this man as one who had been detained in the detention centre awaiting deportation. He watched as the man opened the door of the outbuilding and for a moment glimpsed more men, apparently working in the building. PC Everett had seen enough to realise that AB had been right to be concerned. He started the car and drove away.

A few miles along the road, he pulled up and turned into the car park of the public house. There were only a few locals standing at the bar. He asked the landlord for a menu, decided on a baguette, and asked for a glass of white wine.

Meanwhile, back at the farm, Sherriff was talking to one of his security staff.

'There was a stationary car up on the hill. It was there for some time,' the man said.

'I'll come and look at the tape,' Sheriff replied. It appeared that the man had binoculars and was looking towards the farm.

'We can't risk being discovered,' said Sherriff. 'Get one of the drivers to take the necessary action.'

'I've already got a man following the car and, at the moment, it is parked in the pub car park,' the security man replied.

'Okay,' said Sherriff. 'I'll leave it up to you, then.'

A van pulled into the pub car park and two men left it and entered the pub. PC Everett, who was enjoying his lunch, looked up as the men entered. To his surprise he recognised one of the men and wondered what the villain was doing in this quiet country village. The last that he had heard of Johnny Johnson, he was spending time in Portsmouth jail for GBH. The men ordered beers and sat in a corner of the bar. PC Everett tried to listen to their conversation but couldn't make out what they were saying. However, Johnny Johnson was telling his companion that he had been recognised. They knew that they would have to act quickly when PC Everett left the pub.

PC Everett finished his lunch, paid his bill and made for the car park. He decided to drive a short distance up the road to find somewhere that he could park, in order that he could get in touch with someone at the police station to inform them of his suspicions concerning Woodville Farm and then find out more about Johnny Johnson.

As he pulled into a secluded spot, along a turning off the main road, Johnny Johnson's van went past but he did not think that he had been spotted. How wrong he was! When the men reached the crossroads, they backed up the road that crossed the main route and sat waiting for PC Everett to come along.

Meanwhile, PC Everett dialled Detective Sergeant Jones and relayed his concerns about the activity at the farm.

Detective Sergeant Jones said he would get someone to look into the activities. PC Everett then asked for an update on Johnny Johnson. Detective Sergeant Jones called back saying that Johnny Johnson had not been released from prison but was, in fact, on the run after escaping a month ago. PC Everett was about to give the number of the van that Johnny Johnson was driving when his phone went dead. He decided that he would return to the police station as there was nothing more that he could do.

PC Everett pulled back onto the main road and as he reached the crossroads, he slowed but it was too late to avoid the van that had, at the last minute, pulled out in front of him. His car turned a summersault landing on its roof. PC Everett, although having received some injuries, tried to release himself from his seat belt but he lacked the energy needed and he fell back exhausted. Then there was a large explosion as the petrol ignited and the car was a ball of fire. Johnny Johnson called the emergency services. The two men had both climbed from their vehicle at the moment of impact and were uninjured. The flames now engulfed their van. When the emergency services arrived the vehicles were well alight. It was too late to save PC Everett, and his charred remains were removed from the vehicle before it was towed away. The police took the men's details. Their story was that they were halfway across the road junction when the car had come, at high speed, along the road and they hadn't had time to move out of its way. The car had burst into flames and they had no way of helping the driver. Of course, they had false documents but there was no reason to doubt their story. The police gave the men a lift back to the pub where they phoned for another van to pick them up.

At the police station, Detective Sergeant Jones was about to pass on the information concerning the farm, when he was called out on another job. The information did not seem important so he decided it could wait. In an unfortunate coincidence, Detective Sergeant Jones and a young probationary police woman were driving to investigate a robbery at a local DIY store when their police car was hit by a speeding motor vehicle. Surprisingly, the young PC received few injuries but Detective Sergeant Jones was unconscious. Although shocked, the PC opened the door of the car and called for an ambulance and a back-up team from the police station.

When the paramedics arrived there was little they could do for Detective Sergeant Jones and he was transferred to the ambulance and rushed to the local accident hospital where he remained in a coma.

Meanwhile, at the police station, PC Everett's message, although logged, would receive no action. No one questioned why PC Everett had used his day off to go into the Meon Valley on his own. His wife had thought that he was on police business and she was surprised when she was informed that this was not the case. PC Everett was a careful driver and it was hard to understand how he had made such a careless mistake. Friends drove his wife to the accident scene where colleagues had left many flowers. She visited the pub and spoke with the landlord.

'Was my husband drinking?' she asked.

'Only a glass of white wine,' he replied. 'No one was with him,' he replied to her question.

At least he hadn't been meeting another woman, she thought. If it wasn't police business, what else could he have been doing out in the Meon Valley?

Some days later the funeral of PC Everett, a long-serving and highly respected PC, took place and Sherriff breathed a sigh of relief. DS Jones remained in a coma.

Chapter Fifteen

Greg and Sue were preparing to spend some time with Maggie and Ali. Maggie had just had a baby boy and they were very excited. Greg's brother had agreed to manage Elmwood Farm for two weeks and had moved in with his wife and teenage son. Sue intended to stay with Maggie for as long as she was needed but Greg was going to return to the farm after two weeks. Maggie was looking forward to her parents' visit. It had been some months since she had visited the Meon Valley. She had made many friends in the village, since they had moved from Hampshire, but she would enjoy catching up on the news of old friends. Maggie's baby was thriving and she knew her parents would be delighted to see their grandson. As the day of their visit arrived, Maggie pushed the pram to the end of the drive in order to await their arrival. The baby slept peacefully and didn't stir as his grandparents' car slid to a halt at the bottom of the drive.

During the next few days, Sue and Greg enjoyed getting to adore their grandson and met several of the neighbours. They were pleased to see that Maggie appeared to be happy but Greg had hoped to see more of Ali, who seemed to work long hours at the farm. It was on Greg's last night of his visit that he managed to have a long conversation with Ali.

He had a proposition to put before him, something that he had been thinking about ever since he had received the news that Maggie and Ali had a baby boy. Greg told Ali that he would like to take him on as his partner, in order to expand the business on his farm. Ali was taken by surprise, by the offer, but knew it would not be possible. However, he decided to stall, in order to come up with a satisfactory answer. Fortunately, he had discussed with Maggie his forthcoming visit to his parents when he would be away for some weeks. Maggie and Ali had decided that the baby was too young to travel such a long way, so Maggie would remain in the village. Ali explained to Greg that he would be leaving for home shortly and he would take the time to think about the partnership offer, whilst he was away. Greg was disappointed because he had thought that Ali would be delighted with the offer. Afterwards, he told Sue how disappointed he was but she was optimistic about the final outcome and she said that Ali was probably getting excited about the visit to see his parents and couldn't make such a big decision without giving it more thought.

To Maggie the two weeks simply flew by and it was with sadness that she said goodbye to Greg as he drove away but she sincerely hoped that Ali would agree to a partnership when he came back home. Sue had settled into the daily routine of caring for a young baby and she and Maggie would go for long walks. It was a happy time for them both and they enjoyed the twice-weekly visits to the village hall for the Mother and Baby Group meetings. Everyone in the village was very friendly and the farm workers' wives had been accepted into the community, despite the language problems of many of the newcomers.

As the days passed, Maggie was disappointed that she had received no news from Ali. However, after six weeks she encouraged Sue to return home, as she knew that Greg would be missing his wife. Maggie met Trudy in the village on the day that Sue took the bus to the station, on her way back to the Meon Valley. Trudy was also married to one of the farm workers and it was with some surprise that she learned that Trudy's husband had also gone on a visit to his parents. Trudy had only had one phone call from her husband and she said that she was getting concerned. As they finished their shopping, Maggie invited Trudy back for coffee. They decided to go to the farm the next day to see if there was any news of their husbands.

The following day, as the girls wheeled their prams along the main driveway at the farm, the head of security reported their impending visit to the boss and an alert message went out to the workers. Maggie and Trudy were shown into the office. The manager said he had heard nothing from the boys but they shouldn't worry as the boys would have long distances to travel to reach their remote villages and that communication to the outside world would be slow in reaching its destination.

Wages continued to be paid into Ali and Maggie's joint bank account. When Maggie informed Greg that the money was still being paid, he was mystified. Feeling frustrated about the lack of news from Ali, Greg told Sue he was going to see Sherriff to see if he knew what was happening. As Greg approached Woodville, he realised that there was no activity around the farm. Sherriff came out to meet Greg and they walked together to the farm office. Greg explained Maggie's situation and mentioned that Ali's wages were still being paid into the joint bank account. He emphasised his concern and asked Sherriff how long Maggie would be able to draw the money from the account. Sherriff assured Greg that the money would not be withheld but there had been no news of Ali since he arrived in Northern India, when a short message had been received saying Ali had arrived safely and was travelling, the next day, to Pakistan. Sherriff apologised for not being able to provide Greg with more information.

When Greg arrived back home, he telephoned Maggie and told her that he thought she should come back to the Meon Valley for the time being. And so, the next day, Maggie and her baby son travelled to Elmwood Farm. Maggie had visited Trudy before she left and was told that

Trudy had still not heard from her husband. Trudy said that she was sorry that Maggie was leaving the village and she promised to keep in touch.

Chapter Sixteen

Rosie Page received a telephone call from an agent working in India concerning a terrorist attack on two hotels in the country. Prior to this there had been a lull in the terrorist activity and so this was disturbing news. She called Roger and James to her office to see if they had any further news about terrorist activities. James said that there had been minor incidents but he felt that a big operation was planned and was fearful that it might take place on British soil. He had received information from the police that several immigrants had been reported missing and they had officers trying to trace their whereabouts. Roger said that it was possible they had returned to their homeland but some had wives and families in this country and no news had been received from those missing. James said that wages were still being paid into their bank accounts so they were obviously expected to return to Britain. He was surprised that the wages had not been withdrawn.

In a mosque in the south of England, a meeting took place of senior members of immigrant terrorist groups. The discussion involved details of the plans for the taking over of hospitals in the strategic places, along the south coast. There was a degree of excitement and many expressed pleasure that action was, at last, taking place. Coded details were handed out to the leaders of each group and various points were explained. The aim was for the terrorists to secure the hospitals killing anyone who tried to interfere with the takeover. Later reinforcements would be flown in and they would parachute into hospital grounds. One group would put the radar tower out of action, to enable the aircraft to get through without being detected.

Sherriff and Abdullah discussed how they would break the news to the lads on the farm. Some of the workforce would stay at Woodville but others would be entering nearby towns to create havoc with suicide bombs and car bombs.

AB had read the local paper that gave the news of PC Everett's funeral and also an account of PC Jones's accident. She felt very uneasy and wondered if PC Everett had been investigating the activities at the farm. She thought, no doubt, that someone else would take up the enquiries.

On a beautiful frosty morning AB walked with the family on Portsdown Hill. They admired the beautiful panoramic view of the city and, before making their way back to the car, decided to have lunch at a nearby public house. As they found an empty table, Emma, AB's granddaughter, looked around the bar. In a corner two men from the Meon Valley farm sat drinking beer. Emma was sure that she recognised the men from her visits to the country pub but, as they appeared not to recognise her, she thought that she must be mistaken. They shortly left the pub and walked along the road towards the radar station. They found a place where they could watch the people coming and going without being detected. They had been watching from this spot for some days now and had noted the dates and times when staff arrived and departed. They decided that it was going to be an easier task to take over the radar station than they had anticipated. Once inside, a raiding party would be able to put it out of action quite quickly.

Along the south coast, other strategic posts would also be disabled.

Back at the farm they made their report and there was a feeling of optimism among their colleagues.

Sheikh Hassan was feeling satisfied with the build up to the invasion of the south of England. He had been pleased to hear that the peace that had been enjoyed in Northern Ireland for two years had now been threatened by the shooting of two soldiers and a police constable by a breakaway IRA group and minor incidents had occurred around the world, thus diverting attention from the British Isles. More troops had been sent to Afghanistan and countries in the Third World had asked for assistance. The navy had sent ships to several trouble spots and they had also been deployed in boarding pirate ships operating off the coast of Africa. Because of this, Britain's defence forces were depleted and one officer joked that if Britain's defences were breached now, 'We would need Dad's Army to fight invading troops, because our troops were all overseas!'

In the detention centres, the number of illegal immigrants had diminished, as the courts had been dealing with more cases. Many inmates had been sent back to their own country and others had been released to take up work in Britain. The atmosphere in the centres was more relaxed and it was easier for inmates to make their escape. Muslims had begun to mix more freely with other religious groups and gradually the hostility towards them had lessened.

Chapter Seventeen

When Ali and Trudy's husband left their farm job, they knew that they would not be coming back. They had been ordered to return to Pakistan for more discussions on the roles they were to play. Both men were in good spirits, as they flew first to Dubai and then on to Northern India and Pakistan. When they finally reached the school in Pakistan, where they had received their indoctrination, many of their former school friends were already there. There was a buzz of excitement and everyone knew that soon they would be called upon to sacrifice their lives. The lectures started the next morning and Ali felt he was about to achieve something really fantastic for Allah.

After a week of intensive lectures they were ready to return to Britain but they were granted time to visit their families. However, when they finally returned to Britain they would not go to their previous places of employment.

Arriving in Iran, Ali hired a car and drove along the main highway on the long journey to his home. As he reached the area where his parents lived, he stopped the car and took one last look at the photograph of his wife and son. With a deep sigh he returned the picture to his wallet. Ali's parents had no idea that he was to visit and when he arrived they were overjoyed. A message was sent to his chosen bride's family and the delighted family joined friends and relations for a welcome home party. Ali spoke to his bride-to-be and she shyly welcomed him back home. Their parents made arrangements for the wedding to take place in a month's time and after the wedding ceremony, Ali and his bride would make the journey to Britain.

The day before his wedding Ali went to the mosque to pray. He couldn't help thinking of his wife and child back in England. A moment of panic came over him when he thought about what he was going to do. But quickly his thoughts returned to the honour that would be bestowed upon him and his Iranian family.

In a remote village, in Iran, two families were delighted to welcome home their sons. There were celebrations and everyone wanted to know what the boys had been doing in the school in Pakistan. They didn't reveal the truth about their studies, knowing that after they had performed the task they had been set, their families would be informed of the honour bestowed upon them. The boys had been issued with fake reports to hand to their fathers who seemed to be satisfied with their son's progress. It is difficult to know what their reaction would have been had they known that the boys had, in fact, been in Britain working on a farm and had only spent a short time at the school in Pakistan. Their holiday was to last for just a few weeks and then they would return to the school in Pakistan before flying back to Britain.

Chapter Eighteen

AB listened to the BBC news and was pleased to hear that troops would be withdrawn from Iraq but felt saddened by the continual news of casualties in Afghanistan. Pakistan had bombed the Northern Territories where the Taliban had infiltrated and civilians had been killed. Women and children had fled south to escape the bombing.

Emma came back from a visit to the Meon Valley and said that the weekly darts match had been cancelled as some of the team were unavailable to play. Apparently Charlie, the landlord, was looking for volunteers to fill the vacancies.

'Any idea why they were unavailable?' AB asked.

'Well, some had gone back home to visit their families,' Emma said.

Once again AB began to feel uneasy.

As the days went by with no further news of Ali, Greg decided to make further enquiries and visited the local Member of Parliament during a surgery meeting. The Member of Parliament found the news that two immigrants had disappeared, without trace, quite disturbing so he decided to visit the farms where the immigrants had worked.

As the MP approached one of the farms, the security staff alerted the farm manager, who walked out to the car park to meet his visitor. The Member of Parliament introduced himself and was invited into the office. He expressed his concerns at the number of immigrants that had gone missing and explained that some had come from this farm. The farm manager said it was usual for some of the workers to return home at this time of the year to visit their families, so he had not been concerned. If the workers' wives were still receiving wages, it probably meant that they were coming back. If the wages stopped, the men would not be returning to the farm, probably due to the fact that there was no longer any need for them to send money home to their families. The farm manager was expecting more immigrants to arrive to fill the vacant posts.

When the Member of Parliament arrived back in his office, he telephoned Rosie at MI5 to give her the news and he said that he was satisfied that everything would appear to be in order. He passed the news on to Greg and said it was probable that Ali had another wife in Iran and he thought it unlikely that he would return to the Meon Valley. Greg was devastated and informed Sue of the situation. They were surprised that Maggie did not appear to be upset when they told her that Ali was unlikely to return home. The news seemed to be confirmed later that week when the wages did not arrive and from then on no further payments were received.

Back at the MI5 headquarters, when Rosie Page listened to the news bulletins, she once again had an uneasy feeling. Everything had been too quiet recently with just a few incidents in foreign parts but nothing here in mainland Britain. She picked up the telephone and dialled James's number. Rosie asked James if he and Roger would come and see her.

When they arrived she told them about her fears. The only news they had was concerning the purchase made by a foreign millionaire of a fleet of aircraft. It was thought that the person concerned was to start up a new airline company but there had been no official announcement in this regard. Rosie asked if there had been any news about the missing immigrants.

'No, but the wages are no longer being paid to their wives and we have agents still trying to find out where they went,' said James.

Rosie tuned in to the news programme and they listened to the announcement that the Americans were at last departing from Iraq. Rosie reckoned that it would be a signal for insurgents to move in and she hoped that civil war would not break out. As the newsreader's voice droned on, he announced that there had been riots on the streets of Iran because of the presidential election result. Many Iranians thought that the election had been rigged.

'That's all we needed,' James said.

The newly elected President was now blaming Britain for stirring up trouble. Roger said that the President would probably be too busy controlling the situation in Iran to worry about causing trouble in Britain but, once the situation had calmed down, then security in Britain would be at risk.

The Prime Minister called a cabinet meeting and invited Rosie to be present. As the meeting assembled, there was a buzz of conversation, mostly concerning the news coming in from Iran. The PM said that, as yet, no Brits had been arrested and news reporters were able to report on the situation without censor or arrest, but feared that might change. He said that he would send urgent warnings to firms working in Iran to be vigilant and not to 'rock the boat'. The safety of British citizens was paramount and, if the situation worsened, arrangements would be made to bring the British workers back home.

The meeting lasted for a long time as ministers questioned Rosie about the security situation. Eventually, looking tired and rather concerned, the PM called the meeting to a close.

British agents, Charles and Freddie, were now on their way to Iran, having received orders from headquarters, but they were reluctant to leave Saudi Arabia where they had been delving into Sheikh Hassan's activities.

Chapter Nineteen

AB's Grandson, David, wheeled his bicycle from the garage and checked the tyres. His friend was waiting for him. Both boys were in training as they hoped to cycle to Lands End during a break from college.

'Where shall we go?' his friend asked.

'Let's go down to the Meon Valley,' David replied, and so they set off on their journey.

David had been interested in his sister's stories about the pub's darts team and apparently they now ran a quiz evening. They could get a bar snack and cold drinks when they arrived there.

It was a very hot day and by the time they reached their destination they were exhausted. When they entered the pub they received a warm welcome from Charlie and Bert. The old man called a greeting from his seat in the corner. David and his friend ordered drinks and a bar snack and were grateful for the rest. As they ate their lunch, a low-flying aircraft flew over the pub and landed close by. Bert said that it belonged to the owner of the farm. Apparently a landing strip had been built on adjoining land and there seemed to be frequent flights from there now.

'It has become somewhat of a nuisance,' Charlie said.

Before the boys left the pub, they asked for details of the quiz evenings and also said that they would like to join the darts team, if they could persuade another friend to drive them to the pub.

As the boys reluctantly left the pub and made their way home, another plane flew over. The boys dismounted from their bicycles and watched as six men climbed from the aircraft and walked towards the farm.

When the boys arrived home they couldn't wait to tell their friends. AB listened to their conversation and wondered if planning permission had been given for the airstrip.

Sheikh Hassan was hoping that he would not have to delay his call for action, now that armed forces were returning from Iraq

Could he afford to wait longer? he wondered. Determined that his mission should not fail, he picked up the telephone and set the date for the operation to finally go ahead.

Chapter Twenty

Greg Petersen walked to the far side of the field where his cows were grazing. He had thought that they might be spooked by the aircraft taking off and landing on the runway of the adjoining property and was relieved that they were not showing any signs of distress. However, he decided to drive them to the east side of the field, where he hoped they would be less likely to be affected by any aircraft activity.

Having finished the task, he glanced back towards his neighbour's property. Greg had become quite friendly with Abdullah and Sherriff and Sue and Maggie had made friends with their wives. The immigrants' children attended the local school and their toddlers went to the pre-school nursery, so it was inevitable that friendships were formed. The Mother and Baby Group were thriving and comprised various nationalities and most of the immigrant families had integrated into the community. A few still had difficulties with the language but many spoke English quite well.

As the invasion of Britain drew near, Abdullah had serious doubts about the success of the planned operation. Sherriff noticed that he was very short tempered with the men and he began to be concerned about Abdullah's leadership. As they sat down to discuss the latest plans, Sherriff admitted that he didn't think the operation would succeed. Abdullah nodded in agreement and told Sherriff that because many of the families had become part of the community, they now had divided loyalties.

When Greg returned to the farmhouse, Sue made coffee and then took some newly baked scones from the oven. Greg said that it looked like Abdullah had taken on more men.

'I can't understand how he can afford to do so,' he said.

'Have you asked him?' Sue said. 'I bet its cheap labour. Do you reckon some of the men may be illegal immigrants?'

'I doubt it,' Greg said. 'Only last week he was condemning people that condoned that kind of labour. He is taking some livestock to market tomorrow. I'll ask him what his secret is.'

Maggie was at the Mother and Baby Group and was telling her friends how she was planning the baby's christening. The Muslim ladies in the group were asking questions about the ceremony and Maggie did her best to explain why Christians had their babies christened and decided it might be better if the vicar came to talk to the group about what christening meant. She went on to say that perhaps someone from the Muslim community could also give a talk and the committee agreed that all ethnic groups should be invited to ask a speaker to talk about how new babies were welcomed into their communities. Everyone agreed it was an excellent idea. The gathering was a happy occasion and the toddlers sang a final song, with the help of their parents, before everyone departed.

As Maggie made her way home, she decided that she would invite her new friends to the christening. When she passed the pub she noticed that some of the villagers were going into the main entrance and gave them a friendly wave. Several armed vehicles passed Maggie and she began to quicken her step when she heard the sound of gunfire in the distance. As she turned into the drive of her father's farm, a loud explosion shook the ground. Maggie felt a moment of panic and began to run up the drive.

Her father came out to meet her and gave her the news of the invasion. Greg said that he was about to go down to the far end of the field where the cows were grazing and Maggie decided to accompany him. It was a pleasant spring day with a light breeze blowing and a clear blue sky. As they reached the perimeter of the field Greg glanced towards the buildings of Woodville Farm. He was surprised that there appeared to be little activity. The airstrip was empty and there were no aircraft parked by the sheds. Greg asked Maggie if she thought it strange that the farm looked deserted. Maggie said she wondered if Abdullah was selling Woodville Farm but she went on to say that the women from the farm had not mentioned it that morning.

As they turned to walk back to Elmwood Farm, a plane came in to land. When it came to a stop, the door opened and several men descended to the runway and walked briskly to Woodville Farm. Maggie couldn't believe what she was seeing. The men were dressed in military uniforms. She turned to look at her father and, as they realised that the men must be something to do with the invasion, they began to think that they had been taken in by everyone at Woodville Farm. Greg now understood how Abdullah and Sherriff were able to finance the farm and employ so many staff and Maggie now wondered about her husband. Was Ali involved in the plot to invade Britain? Greg and Maggie quickened their steps towards home. They were both silent and buried in their own thoughts.

When they reached Elmwood Farm Sue came to meet them and was eager to know what was going on. She said she had been scared by the explosions and couldn't believe that people were invading Britain. There was the sound of gunfire in the distance and, as they entered the kitchen, there was a knock on the front door. Greg went to open it and was greeted by a policeman. He said that the area was being evacuated. Coaches would be arriving shortly and would park outside the pub. They would wait for 30 minutes and would then depart. Greg said that he could not leave his cattle but the policeman said that he would not advise staying in the area as it could become a battle zone. After the policeman left, Greg and Sue tried to persuade Maggie to leave with her son but she was determined to stay.

Inside the pub, the landlord surveyed the customers in the restaurant and smiled. He was happy that several of the regulars were eating. So many pubs were losing money but for most of the year, his bar was full of tourists, as well as the locals and personnel from the local farms, who would come in during lunch breaks. As more locals entered the pub he was surprised by the sudden influx and laughingly asked one man if he had been thrown out of his home.

'Haven't you heard the news?' was the reply.

Several of the villagers spoke at once.

'England had been invaded,' they chorused.

The landlord thought that they were joking. He turned on the radio and was surprised to hear a foreigner telling listeners to stay at home and not to resist any requests made by the invading army. Charlie was still not convinced but when four men in uniform burst into the bar, he quickly changed his mind. These men were serious! One of the men spoke. He said that if they cooperated no one would get hurt.

'If you have any weapons, hand them over now,' he shouted. 'Anyone found to be in possession of weapons later will be shot on the spot.'

Charlie looked towards the cupboard at the far end of the bar. It was locked and contained two rifles and four pistols but he had no intention of parting with his guns and decided he would take a chance at being discovered. One woman was crying hysterically. One of the gunmen aimed his gun and fired a bullet at her feet. She fainted and the gunman laughed and said that any more trouble and there would be dead bodies He advised everybody to make their way home before nightfall.

As the gunmen left the pub there was a bubble of excited conversation. Everyone was wondering who had invaded the country and where were the British troops. In the distance there was sporadic gunfire and a few loud explosions. Many of the customers were reluctant to leave the safety of the pub but after a while the pub began to empty, as everyone was anxious to reach their homes. The last to leave was Bert and as he left he told Charlie to take care and pointed to the locked cupboard. Charlie winked at Bert and began clearing glasses. After tidying up, he closed the pub and joined his wife in the back room. She said that news was still coming through about several hospitals in the south, now occupied by foreign troops. Navy ships had been ordered back to Britain and army divisions around the country had been ordered south. In the hospitals along the south coast there was an underlying buzz of excitement among some of the foreign staff.

A few people decided to stay in the village and, as the gunmen disappeared, a convoy of buses, accompanied by two police cars, drew up outside the pub, Greg, Sue and Maggie joined those remaining behind to watch the buses depart. They wondered when they would see their friends again. As the buses disappeared into the distance, Bert and Charlie entered the pub and the Petersen family made their way home.

When they returned home, Greg said that he was going to see if Sherriff and Abdullah were still on the farm. Sue tried to stop him but he was determined to find out what was happening. He told Sue and Maggie to stay in the farmhouse and at the sign of any trouble to contact him by mobile phone. The gunfire still sounded in the distance but it didn't seem to get any nearer.

As Greg approached Woodville Farm there didn't appear to be any activity. The shed doors were still open but were still empty. Suddenly Sherriff burst out of the front door and ran towards Greg stopping him in his tracks. Taken by surprise Greg demanded an explanation. Sherriff told Greg to get back home before he was shot and demanded to know why he had not taken his family away.

Greg said, 'I'm not leaving my farm. You can't win this battle, Sherriff, so what is the point of the invasion?'

Two men came running from the farmhouse and pointed their guns at Greg. There was a heated discussion between Sherriff and the men but they were called back to the farm and then with other men made their way towards the aircraft. Greg and Sherriff watched as the aircraft took off and flew south. Abdullah came from the farmhouse and the two men tried to persuade Greg to take his family away from the danger zone. However, it was soon apparent that Greg was not going away. Abdullah invited Greg back to Woodville Farm so that he could discuss ways of keeping Greg and his family safe.

As they reached the farmhouse Abdullah's wife came to meet them. To Greg's surprise she was dressed in the burka. Sherriff explained that all women would be required to wear the burka and he said that he would order burkas for Maggie and Sue to keep them safe from foreign visitors. Greg was amused at the thought of Maggie and Sue wearing the burka but he could see the sense of the precaution. One of the women asked if Maggie and Sue were all right and was delighted when Greg assured her that they were fine.

Not wishing to leave his family for too long, Greg left Woodville Farm and headed for home. In the distance he could still hear the noise of gunfire and he wondered how far away the battle was taking place. As he reached home the sound of aircraft approaching from the north made him look towards the sky. He was relieved to see that they were British planes. Suddenly a foreign aircraft approached from the south and like a flash, a British plane dived in to intercept. A battle commenced but the lone aircraft stood no chance and it was shot down. As it reached the ground there was a loud explosion and the plane burst into flames. Greg ran across his land to where his cows were grazing but, though they seemed restless, they were all safe. Greg couldn't get near to the aircraft, as the flames were too fierce, but he knew it was unlikely anyone had survived. As he watched in horror, Abdullah and Sherriff came running across their land and Greg walked to the fence to join them. They realised nothing could be done to save any of the men. As they stood in silence, the British planes returned and flying low they did a victory roll and then disappeared northward. Anxious to know what Abdullah and Sherriff were going to do now, Greg invited them over for coffee. Their wives had joined them and they all crossed the style that connected the farms and walked back to Elmwood Farm. Maggie came to meet them, anxious to know if anyone had survived and if the cows were all right.

Maggie led them into the dining room and the men sat down at the large table, a relic from the past when farmhands would come in for their meals. Maggie, Sue and the women disappeared into the kitchen. Maggie took some hot scones from the oven and some butter from the fridge. She buttered the scones and put jam and cream on them. Sue made the coffee and placed the mugs on a tray. As they helped to carry the coffee and scones into the dining room, the two immigrant wives said how frightened they had been by the recent events.

Sherriff and Abdullah confided in Greg that they didn't now want to take part in the invasion plan but that they didn't know how they were going to avoid being involved. In some ways Greg felt sorry for the pair but he could not forget that his daughter had been dragged into their world. He could not stop himself asking the truth about Ali. Abdullah decided that it was only fair to tell Greg the truth. He didn't know where Ali was now but he said that he had married an Iranian girl when he returned home and he thought that he was probably back in Britain with his bride. Greg was astounded by Abdullah's information and full of rage and he made his feelings known. Maggie was alarmed by Greg's raised voice but when Greg told her the news, she burst into tears. She had liked Ali and trusted him. She found Abdullah's news difficult to believe.

The Iranians left the farmhouse and Sue wondered why they had disappeared so suddenly. The Petersen family talked over the news about Ali and Greg said that he would inform the police about the information he had been given. Maggie sent a text message to Trudy, giving her the news as she thought it likely that Trudy's husband may have married an Iranian girl too, as Trudy still hadn't had any news from her husband.

When Trudy received the text message she was heartbroken. Leaving her son with her parents, Maggie walked into the village to meet up with Sarah, to tell her the news. Apparently, Abdul had left Woodville Farm some time ago and Sarah had a new boyfriend. He lived in Petersfield and didn't work on the farm. The new boyfriend belonged to a rock band and played the drums. He travelled round the country and Sarah went with him on his gigs. She said that Maggie should come with them for a break but Maggie said that she couldn't leave her parents whilst the war was still taking place.

Back at Elmwood Farm the milk tanker had arrived and Greg asked the driver if he had found it difficult to get to the farm.

'I came along the A3 to the point where it joins the A3M, then cut across country. I was stopped by the military at one point and they wanted identity and information concerning my journey. They advised me not to attempt to go too far south down the motorway, as there was a battle going on around Bedhampton and also a fierce battle at Cosham, around the QA Hospital.'

Greg said that he hoped that the tanker would continue to call.

Chapter Twenty-one

AB was writing a letter in the lounge when the sound of aircraft made her turn her eyes to the window. Astounded by what she saw, she went to open the front door. There were an extremely large number of planes and, as she watched, men parachuted from the planes and landed nearby, probably on the M3 motorway.

Suddenly the noise of gunfire erupted and the planes left the scene and turned towards the south. The neighbours gathered in the road to discuss what they should do. Some decided to lock up their homes and drive away from the battle. A few of the men decided to go into the nearby woods where there was a bridge that crossed the motorway, in order to get an idea how serious the battle was and how near to the estate the fighting was taking place. AB used her mobile to contact Sally and James. The telephone was answered by Sally, who said that most of the houses in their road were now empty and their neighbours were preparing to leave. James, Emma and David had walked up to the local pub, where there was a contingent of British soldiers with tanks and other vehicles. The pub was still open but there were no customers. So far, the enemy had not reached this point on the London Road. Apparently, further south, a ring of army personnel, surrounding the QA Hospital, was holding the enemy back, with few casualties. The enemy fighters, in the Cosham area, had been unable to join up with the insurgents in the QA Hospital. The biggest danger now seemed to come from the air and several bombs had been dropped in the Portsmouth area.

James offered to collect AB's prescription from the pharmacy and bring it over as soon as possible. When he eventually arrived, he said that there was a checkpoint at the motorway interchange, so he was stopped and questioned, meaning a delay of some minutes.

The men returned from the woods and confirmed James's account of the situation. The general opinion of the military was that the security line would hold and that the main danger was definitely from the air.

As AB's neighbours stood talking, a lone enemy plane flew over and released a bomb. Everyone dived to the ground. There was a massive explosion and the sound of breaking glass, as windows shattered. The plane disappeared southward and everyone stood up and they were thankful that the bomb hadn't dropped in their road. The bomb had, in fact, dropped on the local primary school. No one was killed, as the children had been evacuated from the area. The blast had also damaged the activity centre. There was one casualty. Part of the ceiling had collapsed on the receptionist. Her injuries were not thought to be life threatening. The explosion caused more of the neighbours to leave the area and head north but AB was determined to remain in her bungalow.

In the local police station a meeting of all personnel was called, in order to give them up-to-date information on the situation and to reorganise the force into check beats. All areas were to be checked and leaflets handed out with advice on how to act should the invasion escalate, although it was not expected to do so as the security rings were holding fast so far.

Sergeant McCormack requested the record book from the reception desk and a police constable asked if there was something he was particularly interested in, that may have been entered in the book. The sergeant said that he understood a lady had been concerned about a farm in the Meon Valley but it hadn't been followed up. One police constable said that the woman appeared to be a little eccentric. Silence had descended on the room, as the men remembered the occasion when the woman had told the policeman on desk duty about her suspicion that there were terrorists in the Meon Valley. Sergeant McCormack took the record book back to his office and went through the entries carefully.

When he found the entry, he noted that the words 'After interview no action to be taken' were written down. Going through the book following that entry, he came across a record of a phone call received from PC Everett in the Meon Valley. The message was taken by DS Jones. He then checked the date and realised it was logged the day DS Jones had been called away. He read the contents of the phone call and realised that PC Everett's message was of great importance and might be the clue to his presence in the Meon Valley.

Sergeant McCormack picked up the telephone and dialled the hospital but was unable to get through. He then called DS Jones's wife. She said that when she last visited the hospital her husband was still in a coma but she was unable to get to the hospital now because of the invasion. She had received a message on her mobile phone, from a senior nurse, to say that her husband had not yet come out of the coma. Sergeant McCormack decided to pay a visit to AB. Before he left the station, he went along to Detective Inspector Richards' office and told him about his suspicions regarding PC Everett's visit to the Meon Valley.

Sally, James, David and Emma had cycled to see AB and they were all in the garden when Sergeant McCormack arrived. He told AB that he wanted to know what she remembered about her interview at the police station and why she had been so concerned. Sally and Emma made coffee and everyone retired to the lounge. David told how he had watched planes landing at Woodville Farm and how the landlord at the pub had told him that the Petersons, at Elmwood Farm, were concerned that their animals might be disturbed by the noise of the aircraft. AB told Sergeant McCormack about her visit to the police station and the interview and how she did not believe her information had been taken seriously. Sergeant McCormack asked if she had spoken to PC Everett.

'No, I was surprised to read that he had been involved in a road accident in the Meon Valley and did wonder whether he had been to Woodville Farm.'

After he had gathered all the information that he needed, Sergeant McCormack made his way back to the police station. On his arrival there, he called a meeting of all the senior staff that were on duty. He told the men about his meeting with AB and said that a thorough search should be made at Woodville Farm. He was going to notify the army commander of his intention to send policemen into the Meon Valley and he would go there now and meet with the Petersons and the landlord of the pub.

Some of the villagers had returned to the village now that it looked unlikely that the war would reach the Meon Valley. Sergeant McCormack was surprised to see so many villagers in the pub, as he was aware that many had been evacuated. He asked Charlie if Greg Peterson was in the bar.

'Greg, someone wants a word,' Charlie called across the bar.

'Have you got somewhere we can talk?' asked Sergeant McCormack.

Charlie led Greg and the sergeant to a room behind the bar and called on his wife to take over.

'What can you tell me about Woodville Farm and its occupants?' Sergeant McCormack asked.

Greg told the sergeant about Abdullah and Sherriff, their wives and children and how it at first seemed that the farm was being run by two wealthy men, how everyone on the farm had joined in village life, how the young children went to the village school, how the older ones caught the school bus to the comprehensive school and how the young men joined the darts club and took part in the pub quiz nights and often played pool in the pub games room. They were well integrated in village life. Greg said that Abdullah and Sherriff were still at the farm and he thought that their wives and some of the other women were still there, although others had gone on the evacuation coaches that had taken the villagers to a place of safety.

As they were talking, the sound of military vehicles entering the village broke the silence of the countryside. The column halted outside the pub and Greg and Sergeant McCormack went outside to meet the major in charge of the operation.

'We intend to take over Woodville Farm and use it as our base,' the major said.

Greg and Charlie walked with the major to the perimeter of Elmwood Farm and Greg pointed out the damaged airstrip and the outbuildings of Woodville Farm.

'I advise you all to stay under cover, just in case there is any resistance from the occupants when we attack,' said the major.

Sergeant McCormack asked if he could be of any assistance. The major thanked him but said that he didn't think that he would need the sergeant's assistance in the operation, but he thought that he should reassure the villagers that it would be best to stay indoors until the operation was over, so Sergeant McCormack went round the village to warn everyone.

Greg and Sue watched the raid from their farm but it was all over very quickly. Abdullah and Sherriff were taken away to be questioned and their wives and children were taken to a detention centre and would probably be deported. The Petersens were sorry to see them go. They had become good friends and had, in the end, taken no part in the invasion. Very quickly the army took possession of Woodville Farm and set up camp there.

Just as Greg and Sue turned to walk back to their farmhouse, they heard the sound of an aircraft. It seemed to be in difficulty and began to descend to the old runway. As it landed, two armed men jumped down from the plane and ran towards Woodville Farm. There was a loud explosion and the plane burst into flames. The men had dived to the ground. After the explosion they stood up and continued towards the farm. However, when they saw British Army troops and vehicles they realised their mistake and changed direction heading towards the village. Greg realised where they were heading and used his mobile phone to contact Charlie.

'Two of the invaders are heading your way,' he said.

Charlie went to the gun cupboard and unlocked it carefully and took down one of the guns. He relocked the cupboard just as the two men entered the pub. He quickly hid the gun under the counter. One of the men told the villagers to lie down on the floor. He asked Charlie for the keys to his car. Charlie said that they were in the back room and he asked his wife to fetch them for him. One of the men went with her to fetch the keys and catching the other man off his guard, Charlie retrieved his gun and taking careful aim shot him and quickly reloaded his gun as the other man ran back into the room. The man raised his gun and pointed it at Charlie, who, realising it was either him or the man, without hesitating fired a shot. The man let out a piercing scream and fell to the ground. As the villagers rose to their feet, some British troops rushed into the pub. They made sure that the invaders were dead and told Charlie that their bodies would be taken away. Charlie quietly picked up his gun and locked it back in the cupboard as a loud cheer echoed around the bar.

Most of the villagers lingered for a while, talking about how frightened they had been and calling Charlie a hero and wondering what the outcome would have been had he not shot the two invaders. Sue and Greg walked back to Elmwood Farm, not daring to talk to each other. Both of them were worried for their daughter and grandson. They were surprised when they reached the farm to find that Maggie was talking to two soldiers. She looked rather distressed and was overjoyed to see her parents.

Greg introduced himself, as he could tell that these were high-ranking officers. One of the men explained that they wished to interview Maggie and would be taking her away for questioning. Greg was outraged and said that, although Maggie had married Ali and had his son, she had not seen him for months and had not had any contact with him since he left the country, supposedly to visit his parents. However, despite Greg's efforts, the officers were adamant and Maggie and her baby were taken away.

Greg and Sue stood together and watched as the car carrying their daughter and grandson drove away into the distance. Greg decided to go to Woodville Farm to try and find out where Maggie had been taken. As he approached the farm he found that it was now heavily guarded and a barrier had been erected across the driveway, one of the soldiers on guard recognised Greg from the pub and asked him what he wanted. Greg explained that Maggie had been taken away for questioning and he wanted to find out where she had gone. The soldier escorted Greg to the farm and took him to meet the officer in charge.

After telling the officer about Maggie's unfortunate marriage and his efforts to get information about Ali when he had disappeared, he thought it unlikely that Maggie would be able to give them any information. It had come as a shock to Maggie that her husband might be involved in terrorism and possibly the invasion of Britain. Greg said that he had put his trust in Ali and had offered him a partnership in the farm when he returned from his visit to his parents.

Although sympathetic, the officer said that it was out of his hands and there was little that he could do but he would have a word with the head of security, to find out what was happening to Maggie and her baby.

Feeling dejected, Greg walked slowly back to Elmwood Farm. Sue came to meet him, hoping for some good news but knew, at once, that there was none. Sue had been crying and was red eyed. She felt so helpless. For the rest of the day Greg busied himself around the farm and Sue sorted out Maggie's laundry, putting everything away tidily.

Maggie had been taken to the army barracks, north of Petersfield, where her baby was taken into care and Maggie was interviewed by senior intelligence officers. However, they soon realised that she was unable to give them any information about Ali's recent activities and they had no grounds to keep her in custody. When the phone call came from Woodville Farm it had already been decided that they would have to release Maggie. She was eventually reunited with her baby and transported back to Elmwood Farm, where there was a happy reunion.

Life in the village had now returned to normal. The villagers had become used to the presence of the army at Woodville Farm and some of the soldiers had now taken the place of the farmhands in visiting the pub to play darts and to join in the quiz nights.

Maggie and Sarah often visited the pub and quickly made friends with the soldiers. Greg and Sue hoped that Maggie would not embark on a serious relationship with one of the lads. Maggie, on her part, was not considering having a steady boyfriend.

Several days after meeting the soldiers in the pub, Maggie was pushing her baby through the village in his wheelchair when one of the soldiers approached. As he reached Maggie, he stopped to pass the time of day.

'It's Maggie, isn't it?' he said.

She was surprised that he knew her name. She replied 'Yes, but I'm sorry, I don't know your name.'

'It's John,' he said. 'What is the baby's name?'

'Jonathan,' she replied and they both laughed. 'Does your family live in Hampshire?' Maggie asked.

'No they live in Brecon, South Wales,' was his reply.

'I expect that you miss them,' Maggie said.

John explained that he had just returned from Afghanistan and that before that he had been in Iraq. He had been due for some leave but it had been cancelled.

'It's tough on married men with families but although I would love to go home to see my mum and dad and my brother and sister, it's not so bad for me here in the Meon Valley.'

Jonathan began to cry so Maggie said that she should take him home as he was due for a feed.

'See you around,' said John and he watched as Maggie walked off and he thought how attractive she looked.

It was a week before Sarah persuaded Maggie to go out for the evening. It was quiz night at the pub so they decided to go along. As they walked through the door, Charlie said that four of the soldiers needed two more in their team. Maggie and Sarah joined the soldiers. They were soon chatting together like old friends but Sarah was surprised that Maggie had already met John and was peeved that Maggie had not told her of their brief encounter. Sarah couldn't stop herself from telling the soldiers about Ali and how he had deserted his wife and child and how Ali was suspected of terrorism. Maggie was astounded by her friend's outburst and seeing the suspicious looks on the faces of the soldiers she realised that she was an unwelcome member of their team and with tears filling her eyes she made a quick exit from the pub.

As Maggie walked home, she wondered if this was going to be the reaction from all the soldiers when they knew about Ali. She had not gone very far before John caught up with her and said that he was sorry for his friends' bad manners.

With choking sobs Maggie told John the whole story. She explained how she knew nothing of Ali's connection with terrorism and had thought him to be an honest farmhand working at Woodville Farm. She explained how Ali said that he was visiting his family to tell them about the birth of his son. Maggie explained how shocked she had been when she was taken away for questioning.

When Maggie and John reached Elmwood Farm Maggie thanked John for listening to her and for escorting her home. Greg came down the drive to meet his daughter but he was surprised to see John and felt uneasy and protective towards his daughter but he was relieved when John gave him a friendly wave and then said goodbye to Maggie and turned to walk back towards the pub.

As they walked back up the drive toward home, Maggie explained how Sarah had told the soldiers about her marriage to Ali and how she thought that it would be difficult to make friends with them now. Greg was furious with Sarah and wondered how she could be so cruel to her friend.

The next day Sarah came to apologise but Maggie found it difficult to forgive her and their friendship would never be the same again. It was inevitable that Maggie would meet the soldiers on a daily basis and it seemed that there was little animosity towards her. She was later to learn that John was responsible for their change in attitude.

Chapter Twenty-two

Life in Waterlooville and Petersfield was more or less back to normal. Most of the shops were open, although some things were in short supply and, reminiscent of World War II, queues would form for essential items. However, there was always the sound of gunfire and explosions in the distance and, occasionally, an enemy aircraft would invade the airspace to drop a bomb. There had been some damage to property and a few casualties. Many of the people, who had left the area, had now returned to their homes and decided to stay.

The war had not penetrated beyond the far south of England and was mainly centred in Gosport and Portsmouth. The Haslar Hospital and the Queen Alexandra Hospital at Cosham were occupied by enemy forces and because patients were involved, it was difficult to make progress.

In London, far from the action, the war had very little impact. Occasional incidents such as car bombs and suicide bombers caused a degree of panic and loss of life. In Parliament there were heated debates, as opposition members wanted to know why this invasion had happened and what was being done to bring the war to an end.

As the Prime Minister and his deputy walked towards the MI5 offices, they knew they must find a way to end the war as quickly as possible. They were about to meet the senior officers of the army, navy and air force, together with Rosie, Roger and James, for progress reports. Rosie had invited special agents, Charles and Freddie, so that they could update them on intelligence operations.

Security around MI5 had been increased and barriers had been erected to deter intruders. Checks were made on all visitors when entering the building. Rosie was informed of the arrival of the Prime Minister and his deputy. The senior military personnel and the secret agents had already arrived. The military men made their excuses for the situation, explaining that government cut backs on funding for the defence of the country was a bone of contention and as the discussion began, it quickly became obvious that the military were placing the blame on the government for sending our forces to Iraq and Afghanistan and various other trouble spots, leaving the defence of our country weakened.

The Prime Minister was determined to put the blame elsewhere and wanted to know why the Secret Service had not notified them of the immediate danger of invasion. Charles and Freddie started to talk at once, furious at the blame landing in their corner. However, Charles explained how they had warned of the danger and had repeatedly emphasised that our home defence was weak. He went on to say that it was not much good changing the alert to red, when there were not enough resources to back up the alert.

The Prime Minister interrupted by saying that troops were being brought back home and that navy ships were now on their way to the south coast ports.

'They shouldn't have been overseas in the first place,' said Freddie. 'Closing the door when the horse has bolted springs to mind,' he added sarcastically.

Rosie interrupted the heated argument.

She said, 'Let's not dwell on the mistakes that have been made. We need to discuss the present situation and what we intend to do about it now.'

The discussion calmed down and the combined forces explained what they intended to do. All navy ships and services overseas were on their way home. Both the army and air force were bringing their troops back to Britain, where they would be deployed in the danger zones. Where navy ships were unable to dock in home ports, they would take on board Royal Navy Marine raiding parties, who would carry out surprise attacks on enemy strongholds. The Deputy Prime Minister asked how soon this could happen and was alarmed to hear that it would take some days to organise. The Prime Minister intended to speak to the nation, later in the day, to encourage everyone to be vigilant.

Charles and Freddie were the first to leave the meeting and couldn't believe how ill-prepared for invasion everyone had been, despite their warnings. As the senior officers left the meeting, they were mumbling about inefficiency and lack of funds. Question time in Parliament was a noisy affair, with the opposition seeking answers as to how an invasion of Britain could take place and the present government were blaming the previous government for the situation.

Chapter Twenty-three

Liz Petrie watched the battle from her lounge window. She felt isolated from the world. Many of the occupants of the block of flats had left Gunwharf Quays. When travelling in the lift she was often alone. Liz turned from the window, picked up her handbag and made her way to the door of the flat. She left the flat and walked towards the lift. Liz heard footsteps from along the hallway and she knew a moment of fear but then felt pleased when she recognised a fellow occupant. They greeted each other with relief. The gentleman expressed his sorrow for her bereavement and went on to say how awful the whole situation was but that he had no intention of leaving the area. They took the lift together and walked out into Gunwharf Quays and made their way to Portsmouth Harbour Station.

At the bus terminal they parted company. Liz was on her way to Commercial Road and her companion was on his way to work in Havant. Both the trains and buses were working to normal timetables but there was always the fear of an enemy plane dropping a bomb. As Liz boarded her bus her companion called after her.

'I'll take you to dinner tonight, if you like.'

Liz smiled and said that she would look forward to getting out of the tower block. As her bus departed, she realised that she hadn't felt so happy for some time.

Commercial Road was crowded with shoppers much to Liz's surprise. However, some of the shops seemed to lack supplies. There had been some bomb damage that had occurred during the early days of the invasion. Debenhams had moved its business to its Southsea branch because the shop in Commercial Road had received a direct hit and men were now clearing the rubble. Fortunately, the raid had taken place at night and the only person killed was a member of the firm's security staff. Liz had intended to eat in Debenhams' restaurant, so she decided instead to go into one of the Cascades' coffee shops that appeared to be undamaged.

There was a buzz of conversation everywhere as people discussed the situation. The main concern was for the doctors and nurses and, of course, the patients, at QA Hospital. The hospital was still occupied by a large number of terrorists.

After spending most of the day in Commercial Road, Liz decided it was time to return to Gunwharf Quays. When she reached the bus terminal, she glanced across the harbour to Gosport and noticed that there were two navy vessels anchored there. In the distance there was the sound of gunfire, so Liz hurried her steps towards Gunwharf and the safety of her block of flats. The porter was on duty in his office on the ground floor. As Liz walked through the entrance hall, he called out a greeting and she stopped to chat. He told Liz that there were only ten flats now occupied but he would give her warning if it became unsafe to remain. He went on to say that everything was locked up by 11.00 pm each day, so she must make sure that she was not out later than that and he gave her his phone number in case she became locked out of the building.

Liz was glad to be home and put the kettle on, in order to make a cup of tea. At 5.00 pm her dinner date rang her bell. He first apologised for not giving her his name.

'It's Garry, by the way,' he said. 'Can you be ready in an hour?' he asked. 'The porter tells me he is locking up at 11.00 pm.'

True to his word, Garry was back at 6.00 pm. Liz was ready to go and so they left the building straight away. They decided to eat locally as they didn't want to be late back. Garry told Liz that he worked for Havant Council in the finance department. He asked Liz how she was managing on her own. Liz found it easy to talk to Garry and there were no awkward silences.

At the restaurant, after perusing the menu, they both declined a starter and ordered chicken for the main course and followed this with lemon meringue pie. When they had finished eating they ordered liqueur coffees. It was 10.15 pm by the time they had finished their meal so they called for the bill straight away. Garry wouldn't allow Liz to pay her share and said that he had enjoyed their evening.

'Let us do this again,' Garry said and Liz agreed.

They hurried back to the flats. The porter was still on duty and he wished them goodnight as they made for the lift. When they reached their floor, Garry walked with Liz to her flat. She was tempted to ask him in but they had already had coffee and she couldn't think of an excuse.

He bent and gently kissed her cheek and as he walked away he said, 'I'll see you tomorrow.'

Liz closed the door and walked into the lounge. She felt lonely. The flat felt empty. She looked from the window towards Gosport but it was a dark night and there was nothing to see except occasionally there was a flash of gunfire and the scene was lit for a few minutes. Oh! How she wished this war would end. Liz had given Garry her mobile number but she was surprised when the phone rang. It was Garry.

'Hi, will you join me in my flat tomorrow around 6.00 pm? I'll cook you a meal.'

Liz was delighted but after putting the phone down, she wondered if she should have accepted the invitation, after all, she knew nothing about Garry.

After a restless night, Liz rose early and had breakfast then left the tower block and walked along the seafront towards Old Portsmouth. It was a fine morning. The sea was calm and glittered in the sunlight. Looking out to the horizon Liz could see ships and hoped they were part of Britain's fleet. She hardly dared to think of the consequences if they were part of the enemy's invasion fleet. When she reached Whale Island she turned back towards Gunwharf Quays. Reaching the Spinnaker Tower, Liz went into the café and ordered coffee. There were no tourists here now and the tower was no longer open.

After coffee Liz returned to the tower block. On her way in, she spoke to the porter who asked her how she had enjoyed her meal with Garry. She said that it had been a pleasant evening.

'He's a great guy,' the porter said. And, as if he had read her thoughts, he went on to say that he was sure that he could be trusted.

Liz spent the afternoon on the computer. Several of the emails were from friends wanting to know how she was coping. At 5.30 pm she was ready to join Garry in his flat. She had spent the last hour trying to make up her mind what to wear. In the end, she decided on a casual look and hoped Garry had done the same.

At 6.00 pm she wondered if she should go straight away or wait for a while. However, at five past six, Garry phoned.

'Ready when you are,' he said.

When Garry opened his door, Liz was relieved that he was dressed casually. He had cooked chicken breasts in a delicious sauce and for desert there was a choice from the freezer. Liz decided on rum and raisin ice cream.

After the meal, Garry made coffee for them and then he moved the carver chairs to the window and they sat looking out towards Gosport. There were still several yachts moored in the Solent but the only activity along the seafront was the security forces keeping watch. It seemed strange, as in normal times this area was always crowded by 8.00 pm with clubbers. As usual, there were the occasional flashes of gunfire from Gosport. Apparently the detention centre had been taken over by invaders and Haslar Hospital was also occupied by enemy forces.

Liz was surprised how quickly the evening had passed and she had enjoyed their time together. At 11.00 pm they heard footsteps along the corridor and realised it was the porter making his final checks before locking up for the night. Liz knew it was time to bid Garry goodnight.

He insisted on escorting her to her flat. Before departing, he kissed her gently on the cheek and waited for her to close her door. Assured that she was now safe, he made his way back home.

Once more alone, Liz realised how isolated she was from the outside world. So many of the flats were now empty and the happy tourists no longer filled the area around the tower block. She desperately hoped that Garry would not leave the block, like so many others had done, but she was not aware that Garry had fallen in love with her and had no intention of leaving.

Chapter Twenty-four

On the day of the invasion, Harry Chambers arrived for work early to take over the night shift. He walked to the staff room and put the kettle on to make tea. His pal Bill had not yet arrived, so he picked up the log book to see if there was anything he should take note of before starting the rounds. One item took his eye, it said a rope ladder had been found on one of the walls but after a roll call, no one was found to be missing. It went on to say that the ladder had been removed. That had happened before and he was at a loss to know what it had been used for and he decided that perhaps more roll calls should be made during the day and possibly an extra one at night. When he had raised the matter previously, it was pointed out that this was not a high-security centre and there had been no escapes. He had felt uneasy about this for some time.

When Bill Johnson arrived he discussed the matter with him and was pleased that his pal felt that he was right. The day shift came to the staff room at the end of their shift and said that everything was in order. As Harry crossed to the gate, to report to the guards, a large number of aircraft flew over. Harry was astonished to see such a large number of planes and couldn't recognise the aircraft. He watched as they flew inland and to his amazement bombs descended from some of the planes. Joined by Bill, they stood gazing with horror at the sight of smoke and fire rising over

Gosport, north of the detention centre. Several of their colleagues joined them but they all felt helpless and wondered what they should do. Harry's mobile phone rang. It was his wife. She assured Harry that she was okay but thought a bomb had dropped nearby. Harry and Bill both hurried home, leaving the new shift to cope with the immigrants. There was a red glow in the sky and anxious people stood in small groups, wondering what was happening and also where our own planes were. People were leaving Gosport and the road to the north was full of slow-moving traffic.

When Harry reached home, he rang the detention centre and managed to get an answer. It was Mickey Jones and he told Harry that the Detention Centre had been invaded by enemy soldiers and that all the surviving staff were locked in the staffroom, but they didn't think they could stay there for long. He went on to say that it had been mayhem at the centre and several of the staff had lost their lives. Fortunately, there was a good supply of arms in the staff room, so they hoped they would soon be able to find a way out. Whilst they were talking, the line went dead and Harry feared the worst. He rang Mickey's mobile number and was relieved when Mickey answered. Apparently, the rope ladder was still in the staff room, so they would check the camera screens, if they were still working, to see if there was a point where they could use the ladder to break out of the detention centre.

Harry wished Mickey good luck then he telephoned head office and gave them all the latest information. He was told to leave Gosport and to contact the military forces at Cosham to see if he could assist them in any way.

After locking up the house, his wife joined him in the car. Harry drove towards Fareham and called at Harry's in-laws. They were adamant that they were not going to leave their home, so Harry's wife decided to stay with them and Harry drove on alone towards Cosham.

Chapter Twenty-five

When the news of the invasion of Haslar reached the Prime Minister, he was astounded. He summoned the military leaders to a meeting to discuss the latest situation.

The air force spokesman was the first to speak. Angrily, he asked why we were reducing the size of our air forces.

'Doesn't the present situation show that this is a great mistake?'

He went on to say that there were no young recruits being employed any more. Before the Prime Minister could answer, the admiral expressed his dismay that none of the obsolete navy vessels were being replaced. The Prime Minister turned towards the army general but he remained silent. He seemed to be satisfied with the size of his defence force. The Prime Minister said that he had ordered a review of the defence forces and adjustments would be made, if they were deemed necessary. He went on to say that the situation at the QA Hospital was serious, although there appeared to be no immediate danger to the staff and patients. Supplies were running low and many of the patients were well enough to be sent home. No new patients had been admitted to the hospital since day one of the invasion. Some of the patients had died from natural causes and their bodies were in the hospital morgue. The chief surgeon had asked the invaders if their coffins could be sent out of the hospital via the usual exit for the deceased and it had been agreed.

Rosie, MI5 chief representative at the meeting, said that this concession could prove useful as live patients well enough to return home could be smuggled out in this way. If the number of coffins leaving the hospital was questioned, the deaths could be put down to malnutrition, due to the shortage of supplies and the lack of food. The PM wondered if this would prove to be too risky.

The admiral reported that the entire navy fleet had now arrived off the south coast of Britain and were ready to send raiding parties to the battle points. They would also stop further enemy troops reinforcing their invasion force. This might force the enemy troops inland but the army were ready to stop any attempt by the enemy to come further from the coastal points they now occupied.

It was at this point that the meeting was closed as there seemed little else to discuss.

Chapter Twenty-six

There was a small gathering of Arab leaders meeting at Sheikh Hassan's palace. He was not a happy man. The invasion of Britain had not gone according to his plan, as most of the expected helpers of his cause had not offered their assistance when it was needed. The IRA no longer seemed interested in helping him and the football hooligans that he had been so sure he could count upon, had been of little use when the real fighting started. Many of the Arab countries had monetary ties to Britain and therefore did not wish to jeopardise their relationship with the UK. Some of his fellow countrymen, who now lived in Britain and had been expected to join the invasion troops when battle commenced, had gone into hiding and had no interest in Hassan's cause. Hassan's trained forces, housed in Britain on various farms around the south and east coasts, were arrested early in the invasion and so the hopes of going further inland than the south coast were unrealistic.

At the meeting, Hassan was trying to enlist the aid of all the Arab nations in his cause but he was having little success. After the meeting, he contacted the head of his supporters in QA Hospital. He gave orders for the invaders to move out of the hospital and to advance northwards. He exploded angrily when he was given excuses why this was not possible. He went on to say that the whole plan was in danger of collapsing if his orders were not obeyed. Hassan then contacted the detention centre and spoke to the leader of the invaders there and he advised that the inmates be requested to join them in the battle to take over the whole of Gosport. However, most of the inmates were not in favour of jeopardising their chances of staying permanently in Britain.

Not knowing how to persuade them that they were expected to join the invasion forces, the leader decided to shoot some of the inmates who were making the biggest protest.

Hearing gunfire, the men in the staff room decided that they must endeavour to escape as soon as possible. As dusk descended, they checked the security screens to find the best point for their escape. Most of the inmates were inside the building so Mickey thought that hopefully, there should be little danger. They discarded their uniforms in favour of casual wear from the stock cupboard. It was decided that a few at a time would depart. Mickey James was to be the last one to go.

Watching the escape, Mickey was pleased to see that it was going according to plan. Then he noticed someone coming out of hut three. He sent a message to the two men just about to be discovered and he hoped that they had their phones on quiet bleep. He saw one of the men take his phone from his pocket and then drag his friend behind the hut just in time with just seconds to spare. Mickey watched as the men carried on to the ladder. They were the last two to climb the wall. Mickey looked round the staff room then locked everything up and put the keys in his pocket. He gave the screen a last look then left the staff room. He wondered where the men that had left hut three had disappeared to and kept checking that he wasn't being followed. At last he reached the ladder and cautiously climbed to the top of the wall and then descended to the other side. Mickey was surprised to see all the men had waited for him. They all said that they would go home first to check on their families then they would report to head office. Mickey wished them good luck and hoped to see them later. He found a place to hide then telephoned Harry, who was relieved to know they had all survived so far.

It took Mickey a long time to get home as there were enemy soldiers on guard along most of the roads. Reaching his house he was pleased to see that his car was still in the drive but his wife's car had gone. The house was intact and there was a note from his wife to say that she had gone to her parents' home in Petersfield to stay. Mickey decided to try and get to Petersfield before reporting to the troops in Cosham. He took the route through the back lanes and was surprised that there was little activity from the enemy. He was stopped at a British checkpoint and asked to explain where he was going and for some proof of identity. Fortunately he had brought a change of clothes with him, together with his uniform and in his wallet he had an identity card. He had to wait some minutes whilst they checked his story but eventually they sent him on his way.

Chapter Twenty-seven

When day broke the next day, it was unusually quiet in QA Hospital. Nurses carried out their usual duties but there were no guards to be seen and when the consultants did their rounds at 10.00 am they still hadn't shown. One of the young doctors volunteered to tour the hospital to try and find out what was happening. There appeared to be no guards around.

An hour later, two guards did show up. The chief surgeon enquired why there were no guards on duty.

One of the guards said, 'It wasn't our intention to stay here for ever and we are now advancing further north. However, there are some guards left on duty here.'

The two guards strolled away and there was an air of optimism in the ward. Around the nurses' station, a small group of staff gathered to discuss what they should do next. One of the consultants called the emergency services on his mobile phone and was amazed to receive an answer. He quickly explained the position and was asked to give his mobile number. A call came one hour later, informing him that ambulances would be coming into the hospital, under army escort, to take out patients that were well enough to return home. A team of Special Forces would be entering the hospital at the same time and the consultant was asked to keep the guards under surveillance, so that the Special Forces knew where to concentrate their action. As the medical staff was informed of the action about to take place, they began to make arrangements for the patients that would be the first to leave. Excitement rose and there was an increased sound of gunfire outside the hospital. One of the guards came to find the chief consultant to ask why he hadn't been into the ward that contained his injured men that morning.

The consultant apologised and went on to say, 'We have been trying to reorganise the beds in the wards now that we have so many empty beds in some of them.'

As he was ushered out by the guard, he realised that this was a good opportunity to keep the guards occupied. He took a young doctor and a senior nurse with him and with a few whispered words to one of his colleagues, he handed over his mobile phone.

When the consultant and his two assistants entered the enemy patients' ward, he proceeded to make his rounds as usual. Some of the men were badly injured and really needed more specialist treatment but as far as the consultant was concerned, these men were patients needing care and he did his best to aid their recovery. The two guards followed him round the ward but he was determined to take his time, exchanging conversation with the young doctor and the nurse. The sound of gunfire continued and seemed to be coming nearer. The nurses seemed nervous and one young nurse dropped a tray of equipment making an almighty clatter. The consultant frowned and the senior nurse gave the girl a lecture about care when handling medical equipment and sent her off to sterilise the equipment. Everyone seemed jittery. The two guards were having a whispered conversation.

In the main ward, the patients waiting to go home had been prepared by the senior nurse and her staff. Suddenly the ward had been invaded by the Special Forces, closely followed by British soldiers. The senior nurse explained what had happened and how the senior consultant had gone to the ward that had the injured enemy soldiers in it to carry out his daily round.

The heavily armed troops took one of the senior doctors to show them the way to the enemy ward, but once the ward was located, they ordered him back to the main ward. Meanwhile, patients ready for discharge were being moved with haste to the ground floor level and then out to the convoy of waiting ambulances. The journey they were about to take was not going to be an easy one but the drivers of the vehicles were used to driving in war zones. It did not take long to empty the ward and the doctors and nurses stood around in groups wondering what was happening elsewhere. The soldiers started to secure the safety of the wards that were occupied by patients that were too ill to leave hospital.

Meanwhile, in the enemy's ward, the chief consultant was still conducting his rounds but knew he would have to finish soon or the guards would suspect his actions. Suddenly a group of armed men rushed into the room. The guards opened fire but before they could fire again they had been shot dead. One of the enemy patients nearest the guards grabbed a gun from the nearest dead man and, using a nurse as a shield, made his way towards the exit. The consultant picked up the other guard's gun and aimed it at the enemy, who now had to look in two directions to avoid being shot. The consultant waited patiently and his patience was rewarded. He took aim carefully and the guard fell to the ground.

Soon the hospital was full of soldiers making sure it was now secure. A division of Welsh soldiers now occupied the building. The atmosphere in the hospital was electric. Everyone was so relieved. Of course, the staff hoped they would soon be able to go off duty and return to their homes. A special guard was mounted on the enemy ward and when they were well enough, they would be transferred by air from the helipad to secure prisons to await trial.

Chapter Twenty-eight

Around the country there had been calls for the government to resign and, as the situation on the south coast had worsened, it was decided to form a coalition party until the war ended when there would be a general election. Forming a coalition party would give an opportunity for people from all parties, with particular talents, to become members of the Cabinet. There was a list of ten nominations for prime minister and a vote was taken. The person with the most votes became prime minister and the person coming next became his deputy. They then set about choosing their cabinet from the list of applicants for the various posts. This new government would remain until the enemy was finally defeated. This situation had calmed the nation and although there were some very angry debates at Cabinet level, the change of government was a definite improvement.

The return of troops from world-wide war zones had meant that there was adequate fighting power to manage the trouble in the south of England. The ports in the south were now occupied by British forces. QA Hospital had now been reclaimed and the battle was now taking place in Cosham and the surrounding area. Also, fighting continued in Gosport. The Haslar Hospital and the detention centre were still occupied by enemy troops. However, it was thought that they would not be able to continue their occupation in these areas for long, now that their access to the dock area was no longer available to them, as the dock had been secured by a joint action by the navy and the marines, who were now also surrounding Haslar Hospital and the detention centre. Troops from the Meon Valley were entering the north of Gosport, forcing the enemy to retreat towards the south. The aim was to completely surround the enemy forces.

Chapter Twenty-nine

In a terraced house in East London, Ali's new wife had settled into her new life in Britain. There were many immigrant families in the area and she had made friends with a group of Iranians. The nearby St Peter's Church had been converted into a mosque and so Ali would meet his new friends for prayer. His wife was pregnant and Ali was sure that she would return to Iran when his mission in Britain was completed. Ali would catch the underground train to London each day where he worked in a city bank. He often longed to be back on the farm working in the open air. Although he didn't think about his family living in the Meon Valley so much, he did sometimes wonder what they were doing and how his son was progressing. Recently two of his friends had committed suicide and blown themselves up, killing large numbers of shoppers in Oxford Street.

Soon after those episodes, the police had made raids in nearby properties and he had felt a little nervous. Sometimes he would wonder why he was about to do the same as his friends. He thought about the people he knew and the friends he had made in the Meon Valley. What would his son think of him when he grew up? He felt like escaping from his new life in East London and going back to the farm but then he would go to the mosque and pray. He knew that Allah would be proud of the sacrifice that he was making. Soon the message would come and he knew he would be ready to do what he was asked to do.

As Ali left for work one morning, his neighbour, who had been an asylum seeker ten years ago and was now legally in this country, was about to get into her car. She called out a cheerful greeting. One day she had told him that she had been tortured in her own country and had paid money to come to Britain and how she had been allowed to stay and now she was so happy. She went on to say that everyone had been so kind to her and she now worked as a nurse at St Mary's Hospital.

As he walked to the underground station, a moment of depression descended upon him. Why would Allah want him to kill innocent people? Surely it couldn't be right, he thought. Then he thought about his training in Pakistan but that didn't seem to help. On the underground train, he looked around the crowded carriage and thought one day soon he would pull the cord and create mayhem around him and he would be dead. Across the carriage a lady smiled at him. In a moment of panic he left the train at the next station. He took a taxi to Waterloo Station and made his way to the ticket office. He bought a return ticket to Petersfield.

On reaching Petersfield Station, he noticed that there seemed to be a large number of policemen and soldiers around the area. He quickly found a taxi waiting outside the station. He asked the taxi driver to take him to Hambledon. He had been going to ask for Elmwood Farm but with all the military in the area he decided it would be better to walk from Hambledon. It was a long walk but he quite enjoyed being in the country once again. A couple of army vehicles passed him by and as he passed Woodville Farm he was surprised to see that it was occupied by the army. He walked into the nearby woods and decided to watch the main entrance to Elmwood Farm before going to see his wife and son. He waited a long while but at last Maggie left the farm with his son. The boy was walking now and Ali wanted to rush out and say 'I'm your dad' but an army vehicle came to a halt just at that moment and the driver jumped from the vehicle. Ali's son ran to him and was lifted high into the air. Maggie joined them and John kissed her on the cheek. Then they all walked back to the farm.

Ali was devastated. How could she be unfaithful? he thought. Sadly, he walked back to Hambledon and called for a taxi. As he boarded his train at Petersfield Station, he knew now what he must do. When he eventually arrived home his new wife said that the bank had telephoned to ask why he was not at work. Feeling guilty he told her that he had met up with friends and had spent a day in the country.

The next morning Ali walked to the mosque to pray. On leaving he was handed an envelope giving him instructions. Tomorrow he would blow himself up. He went to a nearby house where he received all the equipment he would need. He waited for his wife to leave home then he entered the house by the back door, wishing to avoid speaking to neighbours. He climbed the stairs to the attic. Pushing open the trapdoor, he carefully placed the lethal equipment on the floor then closed the trapdoor and slid the bolt across. He knew it was unlikely that his wife would go into the attic.

Ali spent the rest of the day working out a plan for the next day. He walked to the underground station noting how long it would take him to walk the distance. At the station he bought a ticket and walked down the steps to the platform where the train would take him to the city. He checked his watch again and then boarded the next train. As the train pulled into each station he checked his watch. By the time the train reached St Paul's Station it was packed with people. He knew this was it; this would be the place where, tomorrow, he would detonate the bomb. He was certain that it would cause absolute mayhem. He left the train and crossed over to the other platform to make his way home. He boarded the next train and quickly found a seat.

Sitting opposite him, he noticed a mother and her young son. They were chatting happily and for a second Ali felt a moment of panic. When the mother and son left the train, at the next stop, he calmed down and he felt confident he could carry out his task. When he reached his station, he left the train and made his way home. Ali's wife was busy in the kitchen and she was surprised to see him home at this time of the day. He said that he had felt unwell and decided to come home.

The next morning, Ali waited for his wife to leave the house and then, after ten minutes, he climbed to the attic, pulled back the bolt and carefully opened the trapdoor. He carefully brought the bomb down from the attic and into the kitchen. He strapped the bomb to his body, and then put on a sweater and his jacket. He inserted the detonator into his pocket. Ali checked the time and opened the back door. Taking a quick look round, he stepped into the garden, closed the door and then walked round to the front of the house. His neighbour called a friendly 'Hello' and he gave her a wave as he turned into the road and started his walk to the station.

In the ticket office, Ali bought a ticket to Tottenham Court Road. As the train pulled into the station he checked his watch once more. So far everything was going to plan. He did get a little anxious when the train waited so long in the tunnel before entering one of the stations but once they were moving again, he felt focused on his aim. He couldn't look at his fellow passengers but kept looking at the floor, occasionally looking up when they reached a station. When they finally reached the Bank Station, he knew that his moment of fame was near! The train moved off and seemed to speed up as it went through the tunnel towards St Paul's Station. Putting his hand into his pocket, he found the detonator and then waited until the train pulled into the station. Then he detonated the bomb.

Ali was killed instantly. Many of the passengers were killed but there were people screaming in agony. Survivors from the front of the train climbed over the rubble to reach what was left of the platform. Surprisingly some of the platform was still intact and the escalators were working.

In the entrance to the station, people were being stopped from coming any further. The call had gone out to the emergency services and the station had been closed. The Central Line had been closed down and arrangements were quickly put in place to escort any passengers from trains that were now unable to continue their journeys. Because of previous incidents, everything was being well organised. However, screams from badly injured passengers were still coming from the carriage where Ali had detonated the bomb. Fortunately, both the guard and the driver of the train were not seriously injured, as most of the damage was in the centre of the train and there, three carriages were a mess of twisted metal and any people that had survived were trapped and badly injured. The guard and the driver had managed to get to the platform and were met by the first of the emergency services. Some of the passengers were already making their way from the train onto the platform. Outside the station, ambulances were already arriving and were waiting to take injured passengers to hospital. Medical staff took the escalator down to the platform and were dealing with the walking wounded and assessing whether they needed urgent treatment. A badly damaged carriage was being examined by the police and efforts were being made to extract the injured passengers. This was, of course, a difficult and traumatic job. A doctor was dealing with the worst cases and administering pain-killing injections to those that he was able to reach. Of course, in the carriages bearing the worst of the damage, most of the passengers would have been killed instantly, but there were a few seriously injured passengers still alive, including two children.

As the medical staff worked in difficult conditions, above ground people gathered around the station entrance. Many were shocked and seemed unable to move away. Others walked to nearby St Paul's Cathedral, to offer up prayers for the injured. A mobile information vehicle was parked outside the station and people coming from the train were asked to give their names and addresses, if they did not require treatment, in order that the police might contact them later to get any information that they may be able to give. A quick check by medical staff and those passengers needing treatment were escorted to an ambulance, or to a minibus, depending on the severity of their injuries. The hospitals had been alerted to expect large numbers of patients.

The Prime Minister had been informed and he immediately telephoned MI5 to find out if any warning had been received. Rosie said that only yesterday they had received information that a large bomb attack was about to take place. An emergency cabinet meeting was called, as it was thought that this was not the bomb mentioned in the warning and it was felt that the Prime Minister should make a special broadcast, following the evening news, to ask the people to be vigilant. He would also say that we were winning the fight with the invaders and that both Haslar Hospital and the detention centre were back in British hands. QA Hospital had been liberated and was getting back to normal once more, now that the invaders had left the buildings. It was true that there were enemy troops fighting in parts of Gosport and Cosham and the Prime Minister would urge the people to stay away from those areas. The enemy were running short of supplies and they had no way of receiving new ones. It was unlikely that they could fight on much longer.

The British Army had a perfect view of the battle from Portsdown Hill and the enemy had no chance of taking the battle up that hill. Occasional raiding parties tried to climb the hill only to be spotted immediately. Some of the enemy had surrendered realising that they were fighting a losing battle.

Chapter Thirty

As AB made her way by bus to visit her family in Purbrook, the bus was stopped at the motorway interchange. This was now normal practice.

Two soldiers boarded the bus then proceeded to ask each person for some form of identity. They questioned everyone, asking where they were going and for what purpose. When their job was completed, one man was asked to leave the bus with the soldiers. He was taken to their heavily armed vehicle and driven away. Obviously, he was unable to satisfy the soldier that he had nothing to hide.

AB left the bus at Crookhorn Precinct and continued her journey on foot. The area was full of army personnel and the sound of gunfire was sometimes deafening. Sally and James called out a welcome as AB entered their house. In the hall she removed her coat and put on her slippers. She went into the lounge and sat down. The windows that had been damaged in the early part of the invasion were now boarded up but the room was still habitable. Whilst Sally made a cup of tea, James told AB that he was flying to Germany tomorrow to his head office. He had telephoned the airport and they had said that flights were more or less normal. Emma said that she and David were going to a quiz night at the local pub but would be back as soon as it finished.

When they arrived at the pub, they were surprised to see some of their old school friends. It was easy to join one group to make up their number for the quiz. There was a very happy atmosphere in the pub, despite the sporadic sound of gunfire and the occasional loud explosion. There was a curfew in the area that had been set by the local police and so the quiz finished at 9.30 pm, in order that everyone could get home in time.

As Emma and David reached their house, AB was just leaving. She had spent a pleasant evening with Sally and James and a taxi had arrived to take her back home.

As the taxi pulled away, AB called out to Sally, 'I'll see you on Tuesday.'

Sally always visited AB on Tuesday, after leaving her job at the local school at 3.00 pm.

The taxi driver said that he was losing money because of the curfew. He had always relied on the clubbers to boost income and he used to make a considerable part of his money at the weekend. He went on to say that his next taxi passenger would be the last this night.

To avoid the check at the interchange, he drove into Waterlooville first and then on to the London Road. There was a queue of traffic when he reached Cowplain because of the traffic lights and the taxi driver began to wonder if he had made the right decision to come that way. When they finally reached AB's bungalow, he said a hurried goodbye and was swiftly on his way to pick up his last passenger for the night.

Chapter Thirty-one

In the Meon Valley, life was almost back to normal but the army were still occupying Woodville Farm. Maggie and John had become firm friends now and when her parents looked after Jonathan they would go into Petersfield for a swim at the local pool or to an afternoon disco. The disco had become very popular now that surrounding towns had a 10 pm curfew. Since the troops had withdrawn from Iraq and Afghanistan, the soldiers had been able to take seven days' leave every six months and John was due to receive a six-month pass. Maggie knew that he would go home to Wales and that she would miss him. She had given up any idea of Ali returning home and knew that if he did, she would never forgive him for leaving her in such a manner. Jonathan adored John and looked upon him as a father figure.

Greg often wondered how they could have been so naive and often had to face family members who said 'we told you so'. He also wondered what Maggie would do when the war was over and John was sent elsewhere.

When Maggie went to meet John on the eve of his leave, she felt quite depressed. However, John said that he had something to ask her and before she could answer he said, 'Come with me to Wales.'

Maggie knew that she would love to go with John but she couldn't leave Jonathan and even if she could go, would his parents welcome her into their home, with her background?

Seeing Maggie's expression, he thought she was thinking about Jonathan. He quickly added, 'Of course, you must bring Jonathan too.'

She said that she would love to come.

'But what do your parents think about our relationship?' she asked.

'They have already said that they would love to meet you both,' he said.

Maggie was delighted and happily they rushed to give the news to Greg and Sue. Although they were both anxious for their daughter, they said that they hoped she would enjoy visiting John's parents and Sue helped her to pack her case.

The next morning Greg drove John, Maggie and Jonathan to Havant Station for the beginning of their journey to Wales. When they eventually reached Brecon Station, Jonathan was sleeping so John lifted him up and carried him from the train and Maggie followed them with the luggage. As she stepped down to the station platform, a man strode towards them and took the luggage from Maggie and put it down for a moment. Then he gave Maggie a hug and kissed her on the cheek. He turned to John. The cold air had wakened Jonathan.

'Hello, Son. So this is Jonathan,' he said.

Maggie knew that she was going to like this man. As they walked to the car park, the man turned to Maggie and said, as if he had read her thoughts, 'You can call me Glyn, everyone else does.' However, she did notice that John called him Dad.

Maggie had never been to Wales before and thought how pretty the countryside was. She knew that John's father, like her father, owned a farm and as they approached the farm she realised why John felt at home at Elmwood. When they entered the farm, there was a smell of cooking and John's mum emerged from the kitchen. As she hugged her son tears flowed freely. Brushing the flowing tears from her face, she turned to Maggie and Jonathan.

'Come and sit down,' she said. 'You must be very tired and hungry after your journey. John will show you to your room in a moment. I thought we would have a meal in an hour after you have settled in. I'm Cerys, by the way.'

After a welcome mug of tea and a Welsh cake, John took Maggie and Jonathan upstairs. The farmhouse was a bit larger than Elmwood and Maggie's bedroom was large with an en suite. There was also a single bed for Jonathan. John's bedroom was next door. It was just how he had left it when he joined the army. His model railway was still set up and in working order. Jonathan was fascinated and Maggie thought that she would have to get a similar set up at Elmwood. The evening meal was delicious. Cerys was such a good cook. Maggie was accepted into the family and she liked John's sister and brothers.

John took Maggie to the Brecon Beacons the next day and they walked up to the trig point. Maggie marvelled at the fantastic view. Cerys looked after Jonathan for the day and when they returned home she said he had been very good. The following day, John borrowed Glyn's car and took Maggie and Jonathan into Newport to do some shopping. As they drove along the Heads of the Valley Road, Maggie was fascinated by the number of waterfalls. One day they drove to the Wye Valley and the scenery was so beautiful. The week passed so quickly and Maggie was made so welcome but it was soon time to return to the Meon Valley. Cerys and Glyn wondered when they would see their son again and very much hoped that he would not be off to Afghanistan again. They had fallen in love with Maggie and Jonathan and hoped their son's relationship with her would continue.

Chapter Thirty-two

There was a full investigation taking place into the London bombing. The carriage where the bomb had exploded was being thoroughly examined by experts and surviving passengers were being questioned. One young lad, whose mother and sister had been killed in the carriage, had miraculously survived despite his injuries. He said that a man at the other end of the carriage kept looking at the ground but that just before the bomb exploded he looked up. The boy was able to give a good description of the man. He also said that he was wearing a jacket, just like the one he would like to have and that was why he kept looking at him. His mum had told him not to keep staring at people because it was very rude. As he spoke tears ran down his face and he began to sob. A doctor intervened and stopped the questioning but the detective was satisfied with the information he had been given. He told the boy he was very brave and then went on to question other patients.

Some patients from the other carriages mentioned that they had seen an anxious man waiting at the station for the train. He kept looking at his watch as if he thought he was going to be late. If this was the bomber he probably lived near that station so now they had another lead.

Ali's wife couldn't understand why he hadn't returned home and was concerned that he may have been on the train that had been bombed. She asked her neighbour if she had seen Ali leave the house on the day he had disappeared. Her neighbour said that she hadn't seen Ali for three days.

As the days went by, his wife became very anxious and telephoned the bank to see if he had gone to work. The manager of the bank said that Ali had given in his notice some days ago saying that he had another job. He hadn't been at the bank since, although he should have worked four weeks' notice. As she replaced the phone, Ali's wife almost collapsed. She couldn't believe he had just left home. What should she do? Maybe Ali had gone back to Iran. In a panic she phoned her father. He thought that Ali may have died on the train or maybe he was in hospital. He told her to go to the police to make enquiries. If there was no news of him during the next week, she must fly back home.

Ali's wife walked to the police station and spoke to the desk sergeant. He went through the lists of people transferred to the hospitals but Ali wasn't among those hospitalised and he hadn't left his address at the scene of the crash. He was logged as a missing person. Ali's wife went to the local bank to find out how much money was in their account. She was astonished to see such a large amount of money in the current account and when she was told that Ali had also deposited a large sum of money in his savings account, she was shocked. She felt very lonely and although neighbours had rallied round she longed to be home in Iran.

At the police station investigations were being made into Ali's background. Some of his profile didn't ring true and information was passed to MI5, in case they could give them any history on this man. Several days later, the police sent officers to Ali's house with a search warrant. His wife was shaken and wondered what they were looking for in the attic. One of the officers asked if she had a photograph of Ali. Ali's wife produced a photograph of Ali and herself taken by one of their new friends. The photograph was the only one she possessed, apart from his passport photograph. When the search was over, the police departed leaving her completely bewildered. The police returned two days later, with men from the forensic department, to examine the attic.

The following day, a photograph of Ali appeared in several of the daily newspapers, asking if anyone had any information about the man in the photograph that had been missing since the day of the bombing of the railway train.

In the Meon Valley, two days prior to this photograph appearing in the papers, a taxi driver walked into the village pub. Charlie had just opened the doors for the day. Bert was his first customer and had been sitting on the seat outside the pub waiting for it to open. The taxi driver followed him in and went straight to the bar. Charlie served Bert with his usual pint of beer then turned to the taxi driver.

'How's business, Fred?' he said.

'Well, the army keep me busy,' he replied. Then he went on to say, 'Two weeks ago I gave a lift to that young farmhand that went missing, the one who married Greg's daughter, Maggie. So I guess he's back home now.'

Charlie said, 'You must be mistaken because he still hasn't returned.'

'Well, I picked up this passenger from Petersfield Station and dropped him off in Hambledon. I was convinced that he was the missing man. Mind you, I did think it strange that he didn't ask to be dropped off at Elmwood.'

When Greg dropped into the pub for his lunchtime drink, Charlie told him what Fred had said.

'Well, he didn't show up at Elmwood, so I guess Fred was mistaken,' he said.

In London, the police and MI5 were going through the latest missing persons' lists and they were very interested in finding out what had happened to Ali. Armed with some photographs of Ali and other missing persons, the detectives went back to the hospital, where they had questioned the

122

young boy. Doctors were reluctant to give their permission to question the child, who was still very ill, but when the detectives said that it wouldn't take very long, they finally gave them ten minutes to show the boy the photographs.

One of the men explained that the people in the photographs were still missing and he wondered if the boy could recognise anyone. He told him to take his time.

The boy looked at each photograph carefully and then he picked out three of them. One was a photograph of Ali. The detective then asked him to look again at the three photographs in turn.

'Then tell me a little bit about each person,' he said.

Leaving Ali's photograph until last, he showed the boy the photographs once more. The first photograph was of a lady.

'How do you remember her?' asked the detective.

'She spoke to my mum and said she was late for work because she had overslept that morning and that she was on her way to the Bank of England.'

Showing the boy the next photograph, he said, 'What do you remember about this man?'

'He gave my mum his seat when we got on the train. He was very nice. He stood at the end of the carriage and didn't get a seat.'

'This is the last photograph, then you can have a rest,' the detective said.

Excitedly the boy said, 'That is the man who sat at the end of the carriage.'

'Are you sure?' asked the detective.

There was no doubt this was the man that had bombed the train. The boy was positive.

Leaving the hospital, the detectives went to see Ali's wife to break the news of his death.

Sherriff and Abdullah were questioned by MI5 agents, in the high security prison where they had been held since they were arrested. Both of them said that Ali had worked at

Woodville Farm, in the Meon Valley, and also at an East Anglia farm, after he married an English girl.

Chapter Thirty-three

In the Meon Valley, as Charlie opened the pub doors the day after the police published Ali's photograph in the daily papers with the heading 'Missing Man', he picked up *The Daily Telegraph* that the paper boy had left in his post box. He could hardly believe his eyes. He read the paragraph accompanying the photograph that said that Ali's wife had reported him missing. It went on to say that he had disappeared from his East London home on the day the bomb had exploded on the underground train and asked for information from the public.

Charlie was so overcome with shock that he didn't hear Bert enter the pub. He sat staring at the picture of Ali and when Bert spoke, he almost fell off his chair and the paper fell to the floor. Bert picked it up.

'My word, isn't that Ali?' he said.

Charlie walked to the bar and poured Bert his usual drink.

Bert was muttering to himself, 'That is him, isn't it?' he was saying.

Charlie wondered how he could break the news to Greg and Maggie but at Elmwood, it was Maggie who first saw Ali's picture in the paper and rushed down the top field to tell her father. When Greg read the paragraph he put his arms around his daughter.

'There must be some mistake,' he said. But neither of them believed that there was a mistake.

John was on duty for most of the day and Maggie knew she would have to tell him about the photograph when he came off duty. He was due to come to dinner that evening. In the village everyone had seen the picture and Fred, the taxi driver, rushed to the pub to ask Charlie if he had seen Ali's photograph.

'Yes,' said Charlie. 'Seems you were right.'

Greg and Sue felt downcast about the situation and had been shocked to realise that Ali, who was the father of their grandson, had been living in East London with another woman, who thought that she was Ali's wife.

In the evening, Maggie waited anxiously for John to arrive. She had fallen deeply in love with John and his family loved her. Glyn and Cerys had invited Greg and Sue to visit their farm in Brecon and Greg had already arranged for his brother to take charge of Elmwood whilst they were away. Maggie didn't have to tell John the news because he had been summoned by a senior officer. The officer had advised him to finish his relationship with Maggie, until there was more information available about Ali's activities. John had been devastated as he had intended to marry Maggie once she had obtained a divorce from Ali. John apologised to Greg and Sue and then said a sad goodbye to Maggie.

Greg drove to the local police station and spoke to DI Richards but the inspector said that he had not received any news yet and the only information he had was from the newspapers. However, later that day, DI Richards was informed that Ali had been identified as the underground suicide bomber and information was to be released to the press the next day.

The following day, the papers told how Ali had bombed the train and how he and his wife lived in East London. When the police called at the house, to confirm the news, they were unable to get a reply and they had to break into the property. The press were already surrounding the property but the house was empty. Ali's wife had taken a flight to Iran the previous day. After securing the house, the police reported back to the station.

In the Meon Valley, the press were out in force when the police arrived to take Maggie in for questioning. Maggie had been waiting for the police to arrive, as she thought it was inevitable that they would want to ask questions. When she arrived at the police station, she was taken to an interview room. There she told the officer who questioned her that she hadn't seen Ali since he had left to visit his parents, in order to tell them about the birth of their baby.

The officer said, 'How do you explain his visit to the Meon Valley, the day before he bombed the train? Surely he called to see you and his son?'

Maggie said, 'He certainly didn't visit Elmwood Farm, although the taxi driver told me that he had picked Ali up at Petersfield Station and then drove him to Hambledon.'

'But a soldier, driving an army lorry, saw him walking towards the village,' said the officer.

Maggie was completely baffled.

'Did you know that he had married someone else?' asked the officer.

'No,' replied Maggie.

'What do you think of that?' the officer continued.

'I couldn't believe that he was living in this country with a new wife,' Maggie replied.

At this point the officer left the room and called together the senior officers. He told them that he didn't think that Maggie was involved with the terrorist operation and therefore they had no reason to arrest her. He told Maggie that she was free to go but that they may need to question her again. Maggie wondered whether her nightmare would ever end.

When she finally arrived back home, Greg told her that Cerys had telephoned to say how sorry she was about the latest developments and that John had been transferred to a unit in Scotland. Cerys had gone on to say that Greg and Sue were always welcome to visit them in Brecon and that they were sure that Maggie was not involved in any terrorist plot and they hoped the matter would soon be resolved.

Jonathan wanted to know when John was coming to see them again and as the days went by, he kept asking when he was going to see John. In the end Maggie had to tell him that John would be away for a long time.

Chapter Thirty-four

Sally and James decided to have lunch at the local pub. It was a bright, sunny, day and they enjoyed the walk. Barriers had been built across the main road and outside the pub there was a checkpoint. Sally and James produced their passports and then they were allowed to enter the pub.

A number of local people and some army personnel had gathered in the restaurant. James went to the bar, to order some food whilst Sally went to find a table. Despite the number of people, she was able to find a table near a window. Whilst they were eating their meal, a large official-looking vehicle pulled up outside and there seemed to be a great deal of activity near the vehicle. One of the army officers opened the door of the vehicle and Sally and James were surprised to see the Prime Minister step out of the car, followed by his wife. They moved among the soldiers, offering words of encouragement then turned to enter the pub.

As they walked to the bar, they smiled at Sally and James. Speaking to some of the soldiers, the Prime Minister said that he hoped the war would soon be over and went on to praise the soldiers for their efforts to bring peace to the country. He ordered drinks for himself and his wife.

After ten minutes, an army officer told the Prime Minister that transport was ready to take them to the front line. They waved a cheerful goodbye and went on their way.

When the car reached the Portsdown Hill Road, it pulled into a viewpoint and the driver parked the vehicle. At this point, the PM and his wife left the vehicle. They were amazed at the fantastic view of the city of Portsmouth. The officer pointed out various landmarks and it was obvious where the fighting was taking place. The PM was saddened by the bomb damage in the Cosham area. As they continued to watch the battle, some soldiers passed by on their way to relieve those fighting to regain Cosham from the enemy.

About 30 minutes later, several army vehicles, carrying soldiers from the battle zone, arrived at the viewpoint. The soldiers climbed down from the vehicles and formed into lines. Their vehicles reversed and drove back to the battle zone. The PM spoke to each of the men in turn and thanked them for their efforts to end the war. When he had finished speaking to the men, they marched off towards South Downs College, where they set up camp for the night.

Just before the PM left the viewpoint, four men carrying white flags came towards the viewpoint. They had been hiding behind some bushes. The officer in charge raised his gun and asked them to lie down on the ground. Two soldiers searched the enemy soldiers for weapons but they didn't have any. They seemed very frightened. The officer called for a van to take them to the high-security prison. When they had departed he told the PM that they had taken several prisoners just recently. The enemy seemed to be deserting their cause in large numbers. Often the men were hungry and hadn't eaten for some days. The PM asked what nationality they were.

The officer replied, 'They come mainly from Arab and African countries. But there are enemy soldiers from around the world. In fact, anyone who felt they had a grudge against this country.'

When the PM returned to London, he put a call through to Rosie at MI5 and arranged a meeting. As he was about to depart from his office, a message came through from the officer in charge of the battle of Cosham, to say that it was now back in British control. Rosie had also received the news. However, the battle still continued in Gosport.

Chapter Thirty-five

Sheikh Hassan was not in a good mood. He reluctantly realised that his plan had failed. A few of his loyal supporters had gathered together on his yacht to discuss what they should do now. One man suggested they should concentrate on taking possession of Gosport. He was unprepared for the Sheikh's outburst.

'Without further manpower and supplies we have no chance,' said Hassan crossly. 'I'm not prepared to pour money into this debacle.'

The gathered supporters were disappointed and wanted to know why the invasion had failed.

'Incompetent officers and useless soldiers,' Hassan stormed. Men are surrendering in their dozens.'

Hassan's supporters began to leave the yacht, as there seemed little point now in supporting a battle that had little chance of success.

In Gosport, a fierce battle was being fought but enemy officers knew that they could not win this battle without further supplies. Food and ammunition were running out and despite their requests for more supplies, none had been sent. Feeding the men was a big problem and there was growing unrest among them.

The trains in Portsmouth were once more running a normal service and there was a happy atmosphere in Commercial Road. The stores were full of shoppers once again. In Gunwharf Quays many of the shops had reopened.

The ferry to Gosport had begun a limited service and the Isle of Wight ferries had started running a service for those who worked on the mainland. Before passengers used this service, they had to show proof of their identity and the reason they were travelling. The detention centre in Haslar was now occupied by the British Army and the security guards had returned to their posts, as there were a few illegal immigrants detained in the centre. There was no fighting in the immediate area but the sound of gunfire could still be heard, to remind everyone that there was still a war going on in Gosport.

Liz Petrie and Garry had become firm friends and Garry had arranged for Liz to meet his family. Now that the trains were again running from the Portsmouth Harbour Station, the residents of Gunwharf were able to travel further afield, although there were many checkpoints around the south of England. Garry had fallen in love with Liz but he wasn't sure if she was in love with him and he didn't want to jeopardise their friendship. He knew that Liz had been madly in love with Rob and his death, at the hands of terrorists, had left her devastated. Garry wondered if he could ever replace Rob in Liz's life.

Garry's parents were living in Hadleigh, Essex, and Liz was looking forward to their meeting. They were going to stay for the weekend and Liz was a bit apprehensive but she thought it would be great getting away from the distant sound of gunfire. The weathermen were forecasting a fine weekend.

As she packed a small suitcase, Liz hoped the casual clothes would be suitable but at the last minute she packed a more formal dress just in case she should need one. Garry decided that if the opportunity arose he would propose to Liz and he had bought an engagement ring that he carried in his pocket. It was a white gold ring with a single diamond stone. They caught a train from Portsmouth Harbour to

Waterloo where they took a taxi to Liverpool Street Station and then boarded a train going to Rayleigh.

When they arrived at Rayleigh they crossed the road from the station and waited for a bus that would take them to Hadleigh. Garry's parents' house looked towards the sea and they could see Hadleigh Castle in the distance from the bedroom windows. It was a beautiful day when they arrived and Liz quickly felt at home. Eleanor and Cliff, Garry's parents, took an instant liking to Liz. Garry showed Liz to her room and left her to unpack. The room was quite large and had an en suite. The window faced the main road but despite the traffic there was very little noise. The view beyond the road was fantastic. Liz stood for some minutes studying the castle and looking beyond to the sea. Then she turned to start the unpacking of her suitcase.

Garry just dumped his case in his room and went downstairs to talk to his parents. They soon put his mind at rest saying that they approved of Liz. Eleanor left Garry to talk to Cliff and then went upstairs to see if Liz was all right. She knocked on the door before entering then asked Liz if she had everything that she needed.

Liz said, 'Yes, thank you. It's a lovely room.'

Eleanor said that she had been sorry to hear about Rob.

'You must miss him very much,' she said.

'It was dreadful at first,' said Liz, 'but I am adapting to my new life now and Garry has been such a good friend and although I'll never forget Rob, life goes on and I am coping much better now.'

The women made their way downstairs to join Garry and Cliff.

After watching the grand prix on the television, Liz went into the kitchen to help Eleanor prepare the evening meal.

Garry and Liz retired to their rooms early.

After a good night's sleep, Liz awoke at seven o'clock and decided to have a shower. She had just finished dressing when there was a knock at the bedroom door. It was Eleanor with a cup of tea. She was surprised to see that Liz was dressed. Apparently Garry was still sleeping.

When Garry eventually arrived downstairs they all sat down to breakfast. Cliff and Eleanor had been preparing a picnic hamper and, when breakfast was over, Cliff drove the car from the garage and packed the picnic into the boot.

'We thought that you might fancy a day on the beach at Thorpe Bay,' Cliff said.

It was a beautiful sunny day and as the tide had just come in. They found a spot on the grass behind the beach huts where they could eat their lunch. After lunch Garry and Liz took a walk on the beach. It was so peaceful but on the horizon were some of Britain's warships, guarding the coast, a reminder that Britain was still at war

Later Cliff dropped Liz and Garry at Southend Pier and Garry said that they would make their own way home. Feeling energetic Liz and Garry walked the length of the pier. When they reached the end, they went into the restaurant and ordered coffee and it was then that Garry decided to ask Liz if she would marry him. He put his right hand across the table and took Liz's left hand into his, sending a thrill through Liz's body.

'You know that I have fallen in love with you?' he said as he gently stroked her arm.

She looked at Garry and her heart seemed to miss a beat and, hardly daring to speak, she said, 'Yes, and you must know that I feel the same.'

Smiling broadly and taking the ring from his pocket, he said, 'Will you marry me?'

'Oh, yes!' she spluttered.

Garry slid the ring carefully onto her finger. They both laughed. Not bothering to finish their coffee, they left the restaurant and took the train back to the pier entrance. Garry called for a taxi as they were anxious to get back home, in order to tell Eleanor and Cliff their news.

Seeing the taxi draw up outside, Eleanor feared the worst. However, when they told Eleanor and Cliff the news, the couple were delighted.

They began to make plans for the wedding but, although a possible date had been arranged, no decision was made, as Liz first needed to discuss arrangements with her parents, who had recently moved to the Cotswolds. Liz telephoned her parents and told them that she was now engaged to Garry and they would like to come and visit them for a weekend.

Two weeks later they motored from Gunwharf Quays to the Cotswolds. Liz's parents' house was a short drive from a picturesque village. As they drove through the village they noticed a church and they stopped to have a look. From the outside it looked quite small but when they went inside they discovered that it was really quite large and very beautiful. As they stood, hand in hand, looking down the main aisle they knew that they would like to get married in this church, if it could be arranged.

They sat for a while in the beautiful silence and then reluctantly left the church.

Ten minutes later they reached Liz's parents' new home. They drove up the long drive and Liz exclaimed, 'What a beautiful cottage.'

As they left their car, Liz's mum opened the door, pleased to see her daughter. Liz's dad came in from the garden and, when the introductions were over, Liz and Garry were given a guided tour of the cottage.

It had been tastefully extended and had a beautiful kitchen, a large dining room and lounge and upstairs there were four bedrooms, two with en suite, and also a separate bathroom.

In one of the bedrooms, Janet, Liz's mum, said to Liz, 'You can either share this room or, if you prefer, Garry can have the room next door, but that isn't en suite, so he would have to use the bathroom.'

Liz laughed and said, 'What do you think, Garry?'

'Well, I guess I'd better have the room next door,' he said.

Liz and Garry had a very enjoyable time with Janet and Mike and talked about wedding arrangements. Janet was a regular churchgoer and said that she would have a word with the vicar, so Liz and Garry went to the church service on Sunday with Janet and when the service was over, they spoke to the vicar about the possibility of holding their wedding there.

The vicar said that he would call later in the day to discuss the matter. True to his word, he came round to the cottage after evening service. He said that the church was fully booked for some months ahead but if they could wait for another six months, he would pencil a date into his diary. At some point he would need to have some talks with them about the meaning of marriage and the responsibilities of both partners.

Chapter Thirty-six

The Prime Minister and his deputy arrived at MI5 for the meeting to discuss the latest events in the south of England.

Reports from the armed forces in Cosham and Gosport said that the enemy had surrendered and the areas had been secured. The remaining enemy troops had been rounded up and transported to detention centres. Rosie greeted the Prime Minister with a smile.

'It seems that it's all over,' she said.

'Any reports from our agents?' the Prime Minister asked.

Rosie passed a fax that she had received from Agent James to him. The coded message read: 'Hassan's supporters have all deserted and I do not think he will continue his quest to take possession of Great Britain. There have been no further meetings. I'm on my way to Pakistan to assess the problems that have arisen on the Afghanistan/Pakistan borders where Hassan's training camp had been based. The school has been closed and the boys have been sent back home to their families. The Pakistan and Afghanistan police seem to have dealt satisfactorily with the matter but there may still be some suicide bombers living in Great Britain and I advise that the red alert should still apply.'

On his return to parliament, the Prime Minister made arrangements with the BBC to broadcast to the nation.

The whole of Britain tuned in to the Prime Minister's broadcast. He said that a special Peace Day would be held the following week and that the coalition would continue in government for six months, when a general election would be held. He praised those people living in the south of England for their bravery in the past months and went on to say that every effort would be made to repair any damage that had occurred in Cosham and Gosport and other parts of the south.

'Lessons have been learned from the invasion and, in future, tighter restrictions will be placed on people wishing to immigrate to Britain. Newcomers will be welcomed but thorough checks will be made on their background. The numbers coming into the country will be restricted,' he said.

Foreign students wishing to enter British universities would be carefully monitored and those seeking to make trouble would be returned to their own countries.

'Britain,' he said, 'had become a multi-racial country and we should feel proud of this and do our best to see that newcomers are made welcome and accepted as new citizens. Citizenship will be taught to all children from the age of seven and they should learn to treat their fellow students with respect, regardless of colour or creed.'

The Prime Minister's speech was welcomed by most of the British public but, of course, there were some that were refusing to accept that Britain was a multi-racial country.

In the south of England life was getting back to normal. The buses were running pre-war services and the shops in Portsmouth were doing business once more. First aid builders were working to repair damaged buildings and the glaziers were busy replacing windows that had been damaged in the raids. Equipment had been brought in to help with the demolition of unsafe properties and the building of replacements had been started. Everywhere there was a feeling of optimism and relief that life was returning to normality.

In the Meon Valley, all the villagers had now returned home and the pub was full of customers each day. The soldiers from Woodville Farm still visited the pub when they were off duty. The farm was up for sale and the soldiers would soon depart. As Maggie walked past the farm on her way to the play school with Jonathan, she was surprised to see Zahra, wife of Sherriff, walking down the drive.

They stopped to speak for a while. Apparently, all the wives had been interviewed at the detention centre and then returned to their own countries as there was no evidence to show they were involved in terrorist acts and most of them had been devastated when they learned their husbands had plotted against Britain, the country they had grown to love.

Woodville Farm was owned jointly by Sherriff and Abdullah and a solicitor had been appointed to sell the farm, with the proceeds to be confiscated and paid into a victim support charity. Some of the wives had returned to Britain and had been granted permission to retrieve their own possessions. Many had decided to remain in Britain and permission had been granted for them to do so.

Zahra was pleased to see Maggie and said how sorry she was for the devastation that her husband and other farmhands had caused. She went on to say that she had never suspected Ali or any of the other workers of anything so awful. The two of them hugged each other and then Zahra went on to say that she was now working at a restaurant in Petersfield, and that she and Rana had applied for jobs as care workers and hoped that they would soon be employed. Their children were back at school and were very happy. Maggie told Zahra about John and how he had been transferred to Scotland.

The two women made arrangements to meet up again and to keep in touch.

When Maggie arrived home, Greg said that Glyn had phoned to say that John had been sent to Afghanistan for six months. Maggie's heart sank. She told her father that

Woodville was up for sale and then went on to tell him about Zahra and Rana.

Later in the day Maggie telephoned Glyn to tell him about Woodville Farm and to ask him to send her good wishes to John.

Several days later, Glyn telephoned Greg to ask if he and Cerys could come and stay for a few days. Greg was delighted but surprised that they would be coming to Elmwood at Glyn's busiest time on his farm. Sue and Maggie were pleased that Glyn and Cerys were coming to stay and were very much looking forward to the visit.

When Glyn and Cerys arrived at Elmwood, Glyn and Greg made their excuses to Maggie and Cerys and went to have a look round the farm. As they reached the boundary joining Woodville Farm, they stood looking over the fence towards the airstrip.

Greg said, 'I wonder who will purchase Woodville?'

Glyn replied, 'I'm due to look over the farm tomorrow.'

'Are you thinking of selling your farm?' Greg asked.

'No,' replied Glyn. 'If the price is right, I'm going to make an offer. I'm thinking of putting a manager there until John comes out of the army.'

Greg was delighted and hoped that the purchase would go ahead.

The next day, Glyn visited Woodville and toured the farm. He could see that there was good potential and he asked his solicitor to make an offer on his behalf. The first offer was rejected but after making a higher offer it was accepted. Glyn told Greg that he had decided to put John's younger brother in charge of the necessary improvements and John and his brother would later run the farm together. It was decided that the outbuildings would be converted into stables and eventually a riding school would be opened.

Glyn discussed with Greg what he should do with the airstrip. Permanent use might disturb the animals but perhaps it could be used occasionally or would it be better to grass over the airstrip? It was decided to leave a decision until the farm alterations had been made.

Maggie listened anxiously to the news from Afghanistan and was pleased that much progress had been made. The number of troops serving there had been reduced and most of the country was controlled by its own army. Casualty numbers were down and the nation was, on the whole, peaceful.

Chapter Thirty-seven

As Peace Day drew near, excitement grew throughout the country. Many had decorated their streets with bunting and decided to hold street parties for the children. Union flags were flying from buildings across the nation and in the Meon Valley Charlie and his wife were busy organising the arrangements for the village children's party. The Prime Minister had given orders for Downing Street to be decorated and invitations to the party that was to be held there had been sent to a number of children that were acting as a carer to a parent.

When the day arrived, the church bells rang out with joy. The sun shone and it was a glorious day.

Liz and Garry watched as crowds gathered in Gunwharf Quays. Many of the restaurants were serving special party food. There was a long queue for the Spinnaker Tower.

Garry turned to Liz and said, 'Back to normal, then.'

Liz laughed and replied, 'Well, not really. I don't think I've seen this many people here before. Shall we go and join in the fun?'

It was such a happy atmosphere and as darkness fell the sky lit up with fireworks, launched from the navy ships guarding the coast.

Around Britain, nightfall was like New Year's Eve as the fireworks filled the sky once more.

AB and her family stood at the top of Portsdown Hill and watched the display of fireworks in King George V Recreation Ground. The sound of fireworks went on until the early hours of the following morning.

It was astonishing how quickly the damaged buildings were repaired and it wasn't long before new buildings were being planned for the sites where homes and shops had been completely demolished. Those people still homeless had been housed in temporary accommodation that had been installed on various sites.

Chapter Thirty-eight

Six months later, the army had gone from the Meon Valley and John's brother was now occupying Woodville Farm. He was a regular visitor to Elmwood and often sought Greg's advice. John was due to come back to Scotland in the next month or two. Maggie secretly hoped that he would visit his brother at Woodville when he was granted leave.

There had been many acts of bravery during the war and a special medal was being minted for those who had performed such acts. AB was surprised to receive notification from the palace that she was to be awarded a medal for her action in endeavouring to warn the police of the danger to Britain. Another surprised recipient was Charlie, landlord of the Meon Valley pub. The award was for his bravery in shooting dead two of the enemy soldiers. PC Everett was to receive a posthumous award. Among others that received awards for acts of bravery were the guards at the Haslar Detention Centre.

Liz and Garry had been busy planning their wedding. They had paid several visits to the Cotswolds to meet with the vicar, as he had requested. Now they were making arrangements to sell one of the flats. They had decided that they would sell Liz's flat. There had been several interested buyers and it was hoped the sale would take place soon after their wedding.

A date had been set for a general election. The Prime Minister was wondering if he would still be living in Number 10 after the results were announced. He was already making arrangements for a move, should he no longer remain in office. As election day drew nearer there was an air of excitement throughout the country. Some politicians were already making speeches condemning the fact that Britain had been ill prepared for war and others were praising the present government for the successful end to the invasion. Zahra and Rana both thought that it was wonderful that people were able to express their thoughts without fear of arrest, although racism was still frowned upon. They were delighted that they would be allowed to vote.

In Scotland, John had been granted leave and he hired a car for three weeks. He left camp early in the morning and journeyed to Wales. He took several breaks on the way to Brecon and arrived in the late afternoon. His parents were delighted to see him and soon gave him all the news concerning Woodville Farm. John told his parents that, although he had three weeks leave, he intended to spend some time at Woodville as he hoped to convince Maggie to marry him. Although they were naturally disappointed that he would be going away, Glyn and Cerys understood the reason he was going to the Meon Valley and they wished him luck.

John spent a few days at home and then started his journey to Hampshire. As he crossed the Severn Bridge he began to have doubts. What if Maggie had met someone else? Perhaps she wouldn't want to marry him. He tried to think more positive thoughts and increased his speed, anxious to know how Maggie felt about him.

When he reached Chievely, he turned off the M4 onto the A34, then passing through Newbury, he continued his journey, stopping for a short break at Sutton Scotney. He phoned his brother to let him know that he would be with him during the next hour. Continuing his journey he turned

146

onto the A272 heading for Petersfield. His mood had changed and he felt more positive. He loved the Hampshire scenery and he was looking forward to his stay at Woodville. He always enjoyed his brother's company and the prospect of running the farm together was an exciting one.

As he drove up the drive of Woodville, his brother Malcolm opened the door of the farmhouse to come and greet him. When they entered the house, there was a smell of cooking coming from the kitchen and a woman opened the kitchen door to tell them that dinner would be served in 30 minutes. Malcolm introduced Kathleen.

'She generally cooks in the evening for me,' Malcolm said. 'I'll show you to your bedroom. It's the largest one of the four but, as you are hoping to share it with Maggie, I thought it best that you should have that one.'

John liked the room. It had a view across the fields to Elmwood Farm and from a side window you could see the stables, although there were no animals there as yet. After a shower and a change from his uniform, John joined his brother downstairs. When they had finished dinner, they spent the evening discussing plans for the farm. Kathleen wished them goodbye and said she would be over again tomorrow. John was impressed with the work that Malcolm had done so far and asked him what the next step was to be.

'I think that I'm ready to get some animals but I'll need to employ some men first. Greg has offered to help me choose the best stock and I don't think I'll have any problems employing farmhands.'

Over at Elmwood, Greg had watched as John's car drove into Woodville Farm yard.

Not recognising the vehicle, he said to Sue, 'I think that Malcolm has a visitor. Strange that he never said he was expecting someone.'

The next morning, as he opened the curtains in their bedroom, he noticed that the car was still parked in Woodville yard.

Downstairs Maggie was busy preparing Jonathan's breakfast. She had arranged to take him to a friend's house to play with her son. After breakfast, Jonathan, who was anxious to go to his friend's house, was waiting outside for his mother.

Suddenly he rushed into the farmhouse calling, 'Mum, Mum! It's John, it's John!'

Not daring to believe him, she said, 'No, Jonathan, I told you that John had gone away.'

Jonathan stamped his foot.

'It is him, it is!' he said.

She went outside and glanced down the road. Before she could stop him, Jonathan went running down the road at full pelt. Maggie couldn't believe her eyes. John lifted Jonathan up and walked towards Maggie.

Jonathan was saying, 'I told you so, I told you so,' to Maggie.

They all went into Elmwood Farm. Sue and Greg had just sat down to breakfast but they were delighted to see John. He told them that he was on leave and wanted to see Maggie.

'I went home first,' he said, 'but when I explained to Mum and Dad that I wanted to see Maggie, they were very pleased.'

Maggie explained that she had to take Jonathan to play with his friend. Jonathan wanted to stay but John told him to go and play with his friend and he would come with Maggie to fetch him at lunchtime.

As Jonathan went on his way with Maggie, he called out to John, 'You will come back?'

'I certainly will,' John replied.

Later, when Maggie arrived back, they went for a walk through the village and stopped for a drink at the pub. John went in to get the drinks while Maggie found a table outside.

Inside the pub, John received a warm welcome from everyone and Charlie said that the drinks were on him. When John joined Maggie in the garden with the drinks, she told him all the latest village news and it was as if they had never been apart. They stayed talking until it was time to collect Jonathan. Together they walked to Woodville Farm where John drove the car onto the drive. Malcolm was talking to Maggie and she had explained to him that they were going to collect Jonathan from his friend's house. When John joined them he said to Malcolm that he was taking Maggie and Jonathan out for lunch. As Malcolm watched them driving away, he knew that they were very much in love.

Jonathan was waiting anxiously at the front of his friend's house.

'I thought you weren't coming,' he said.

'We had to go back for your seat,' Maggie replied.

John only drove them for a short distance and they turned into the entrance to the Queen Elizabeth the Second Country Park. John parked the car and they walked to the restaurant. They ordered food and drinks and then found a table. When they finished their lunch they went back to the car and John drove them to the top of the hill where they left the car whilst they continued on foot. Maggie hadn't been walking there since before the war and Jonathan had never been there before. John remembered patrolling there when he was stationed in the Meon Valley.

They occasionally stopped to admire the views and Jonathan tried rolling down slopes. This involved John chasing after him before he rolled too far. All too soon, it was time to leave. John left Maggie and Jonathan at Elmwood Farm and, as Jonathan ran up the drive, Maggie thanked John.

He said, 'If you can get Greg and Sue to look after Jonathan tomorrow night, I'd like to take you for a meal in Gunwharf Quays.'

Then he continued on his way to Woodville. Jonathan ran to tell Greg and Sue about his visit to Queen Elizabeth Country Park.

John and Malcolm spent the next morning discussing plans for the farm. They intended to have sheep and cows and Malcolm intended to buy some dairy cows first, so that he could sell the milk to give him an income. He had already had interest from several people wanting to rent the stables and one of the fields to set up a riding school and, after going through the offers with John, they both agreed to accept an offer from someone living in the village, even though it wasn't the best offer. Malcolm was going to advertise for workers but would start with a small number and Glyn had promised to lend him two of his experienced farmhands to begin with. John said that he was sorry that he could not be at Woodville to help in the initial set up but, as soon as he could leave the army, he would join his brother at Woodville.

In the evening, John drove up to Elmwood and found Maggie waiting for him. As they drove out of the village, John headed for the A3M and they were soon on their way to Gunwharf Quays. John told Maggie about the plans for Woodville Farm. Maggie was excited about his news and secretly hoped that he would soon leave the army. Gunwharf Quays was very busy and people were queuing outside the restaurants but John had booked a table, so they were able to go straight in.

The meal was excellent and after leaving the restaurant they stood looking out to sea. There was a full moon with thousands of stars twinkling in the clear night sky. Boats in the harbour were bobbing up and down in the gently lapping sea. It was a truly romantic scene.

John put his arm around Maggie and she snuggled closer to him. She felt so happy. He looked at her and thought how beautiful she was tonight. Completely oblivious of those around them, John pulled her close to him and kissed her firmly on her mouth.

As they breathlessly broke away from each other John said, 'Will you marry me?'

Without any hesitation, she said, 'Yes, I will.'

Then John took a ring from his pocket and placed it on her finger. Hand in hand they walked to the car park and were soon on their way to the Meon Valley.

Greg and Sue were delighted with John and Maggie's news and, after spending two weeks at Woodville, John suggested that Maggie and Jonathan should come to Brecon with him, so that they could break the news to Glyn and Cerys before he headed back to Scotland.

They travelled to Brecon the next day. There were arrangements for the wedding to be made and John and Maggie hoped that they could get married when John had his next leave. Of course, Maggie was hoping that they could get married in the Meon Valley but she wondered how Glyn and Cerys would feel about not having the wedding in Brecon. However, to her surprise, Cerys suggested the Meon Valley would be the best venue. Cerys and Glyn were so pleased and they hoped that it would not be long before John was able to leave the forces.

In fact, the news that he was to leave the army came sooner than expected. There had been a review of the defence forces and army personnel were asked to submit requests for termination of their service. John submitted the necessary forms and was told that he would be able to leave the army in three months. Feeling elated, he sent a text message to Maggie, to tell her the good news and so the arrangements for the wedding began.

Invitations were sent to friends and relations and a two-week honeymoon was booked in the Seychelles. The vicar said that he was glad that they were to get married in the Meon Valley and that he would be happy to officiate. Greg and Sue were going to care for Jonathan whilst the couple were on their honeymoon.

And so, at last, the wedding day arrived.

As Greg walked his daughter down the aisle, he felt very proud of her and thought how beautiful she looked. He knew she was going to be happy with John and that she would soon put the past behind her. John turned to smile at Maggie as she joined him at the altar. The congregation consisted of friends from different cultures and relations from both families.

After the service everyone joined the families in the grounds of Elmwood Farm where a marquee had been erected. It was a happy occasion but one person was heard to say, 'Thank goodness she has married one of our own this time.'

He was asked to leave and told that he wasn't welcome at this celebration. As he was leaving, a resounding cheer echoed around the grounds.

Glyn turned to Greg and said, 'Thank God there are few around like him anymore.'

Maggie and John left the reception during the evening, after saying goodbye to Jonathan. They had hugged him close and told him to be a good boy for his grandparents. Then the taxi drove them away.

The celebrations went on until the morning and gradually the partygoers left. Glyn and Cerys were staying at Woodville for a few days and, after saying goodnight they left with Malcolm. Jonathan had fallen asleep on the sofa, so Greg picked him up and carried him up to bed. It had been a wonderful day and Greg knew that Maggie was going to be very happy.

Chapter Thirty-nine

Life had returned to normal for AB and her family and the worries and hardships of wartime Britain began to fade away.

As she left the bus at Crookhorn Lane, she crossed the road and, walking past the shops, she made her way down the hill to Saint John's Road. She quickened her steps as she walked through the alleyways. She was anxious to find out all the latest news.

Turning into the close, she was pleased to see that all the windows, damaged during the war, had now been replaced and there was no sign that any of the houses needed repairing. AB stood for a moment and enjoyed the silence. No sound of gunfire. Then, suddenly, the silence was broken by the children who were playing football, a sound that had been missing from the close for a long while. Yes, she thought, things were back to normal.

Reaching her family's house, she was greeted by David.

'Hi, Nan. What have you been doing this week? Caught any terrorists lately?'

AB laughed and was about to enter the house when the neighbours all started cheering. Sally said that they had read that AB was to receive an award in the news. Emma began to tell her all about the new boyfriend and how she was now engaged. They had moved into a flat together and were beginning to settle in to their new environment.

AB spent the evening with her family then, at nine o'clock, she phoned for a taxi to take her back home.

The next day was going to be a special day. Her son-in-law was going to drive AB and Sally to Buckingham Palace, as the Queen was going to present bravery medals to some of those that had been selected to receive awards.

As they reached the palace, James was allowed to drive through the gates. AB felt nervous but very proud when they joined some of the others waiting to receive their medals. The Queen smiled as AB stood before her.

She said, 'Well done. Your information was of considerable help, I am told.'

AB thanked the Queen and returned to her seat whilst others collected their medals.

After leaving the building, they stood in front of the palace to have their photographs taken. Leaving the palace, at last, James drove down The Mall, where a large crowd had gathered. They were shouting and cheering and waving flags. It was a wonderful atmosphere.

AB turned to her family and said, 'This is what being British is like. Let's go home and celebrate.'